TASTE

(a *Take It Off* novel)

One taste is never enough…

Spencer Waller's main purpose in life is to protect and serve. After spending years in the military, he gets a coveted spot on the Secret Service detail protecting the president. Spence doesn't have time for women or all the work having a relationship with one requires. But just because he isn't looking for a lady doesn't mean he can't appreciate a beautiful one when he sees her.

And he makes it a point to see one in particular every single day.

Elle Bond has literally chopped and fried her way to the top of the food chain. Earning a coveted position in the White House as the president's personal chef, she figures her professional life can only get better. Her personal life, on the other hand, could use a little bit of an overhaul, and because of that, she tries to ignore the charm-dripping cookie thief every time he comes into her kitchen. After all, she knows better than anyone that just one taste of something good is never enough.

One night after work, Elle is assaulted, threatened, and given an ultimatum. She can't go to the police, and she sure as hell can't do what she was ordered.

But she has to. Or else.

Pale, shaken, and scared to death, Elle confides in Spence, and his protective instincts take over. Together, Elle and Spencer have to uncover a sinister plot and stop it before someone ends up dead.

TASTE

Take It Off Series

CAMBRIA HEBERT

Published by: Cambria Hebert Books, LLC

Your key to escape

http://www.cambriahebert.com

Interior design and typesetting by Sharon Kay
Cover design by MAE I DESIGN
Edited by Cassie McCown
Copyright 2014 by Cambria Hebert

ISBN: 978-1-938857-54-6

Other books by Cambria Hebert

Heven and Hell Series
Before
Masquerade
Between
Charade
Bewitched
Tirade
Beneath
Renegade
Heven & Hell Anthology

Death Escorts
Recalled
Charmed

Take It Off
Torch
Tease
Tempt
Text
Tipsy
Tricks
Tattoo
Tryst

Distant Desires Serial
(erotic)
Part One
Part Two
Part Three (conclusion)

TASTE

"Home is any four walls that enclose the right person."
—Helen Rowland

1

I was restless. Even after a full day of work and the feeling of exhaustion cloaking my limbs, I still couldn't fall asleep. There was a recipe, a few ideas for new dishes to try, and the beginnings of a big menu plan I needed to write cluttering up my mind. I knew it was likely the reason I was still lying here staring at the ceiling.

Sigh…

I sent the covers flying back, kicking my legs free, and climbed out of bed. With one last lingering, yearning glance at my pillow, I turned away and quietly made my way down to the kitchen.

Once there, I pulled out my notebook and black pen to jot down all the competing thoughts and ideas. They were good ideas, great ingredient combinations and a solid start to the menu. Too bad I couldn't think of this stuff during the day, say, when I wasn't supposed to be sleeping.

Of course, my day was so filled with everything else that it really wasn't that surprising these ideas only came after the lights were out and I was blessed with moments of quiet silence.

As I pondered a new sauce for a rack of lamb, I worked on autopilot, brewing a cup of hot chamomile tea. Perhaps its relaxing herbs and heat would be the remedy I needed to rest tonight.

I reached into the overhead cabinet for the tea bags, and my eyes landed on the cookies. A smile immediately stole over my features, causing me to stand there in the center of the kitchen, grinning in the middle of the night, alone, like a complete idiot.

I couldn't see a cookie these days and not think of Spencer. His charm was like a stealth ninja and so was his ability to blindside my mind with thoughts of him. He was only the second man I'd ever met in my entire life who could completely take over the inside of my head.

But it didn't matter how much he grinned, how much he teased me, and how many of my cookies he managed to stuff into his mouth at once; I couldn't let him in my life.

The first guy who ever took over my thoughts taught me that.

I was just now getting my life where I wanted it to be after the disarray he left behind.

But oh, Spence was tempting. With dark-blond hair that always looked like it was just a little too long and needed trimming, short sideburns that hugged the side of his striking face… I couldn't really call Spencer handsome. He was too rough around the edges for that. He had strong, dark eyebrows that slashed over honey-colored eyes, full lips that could draw into an intimidating line, and a strong nose that appeared to have been broken a time or two.

His body also looked like it had been through a couple of battles. He boasted wide shoulders, thick arms, and a tapered waist that was always accentuated by the tailored black suit he had to wear.

It just proved that clothes did not make the man. Spence made his clothes. Hell, he *owned* them. As a Secret Service operative, I think Spencer was supposed to look professional and quiet, sort of like he could blend in anywhere.

I have no idea how the hell he got his job because nothing about him blended in. He drew eyes like fireworks in a pitch-black sky. I mean, every time he waltzed into the kitchen, every pot on the stove was in danger of being burnt up because none of the staff could concentrate.

As if to prove my point, the teakettle whistled angrily, the shrill sound snapping me out of my daydreaming and making me wince. Quickly, I yanked the kettle off the burner and poured the boiling water over a bag into a ceramic mug. Steam rose from the top in great puffs, and I shook my head, annoyed I let the water boil that heavily. I'd have to wait forever for this tea to cool enough to drink.

I carried the mug a few steps to the tiny island in the center of the kitchen and set it beside my notebook. The perfect herb to add to the crust on the lamb popped into my head and I hurried to jot it down.

The room was completely silent except for the light scrawling of my pen across paper. Maybe that's why I heard the sound.

It was a low scraping sound, like wood rubbing against wood. I tilted my head, confused. It was an odd sound to hear in the middle of the night, something I might not even think twice about if it were daylight.

But it wasn't.

A muffled thump overhead caused my entire body to tighten like a shoelace with a double knot. My head snapped back to stare up at the ceiling.

I was being crazy.

I was being paranoid.

Thump.

There was someone in the apartment!

A surge of adrenaline so powerful it blurred my vision for a few seconds rocketed through me. My brain tried to think as my body went into overdrive. That first sound, someone had opened a window upstairs. The thump was when that someone dropped their up-to-no-good ass into my house.

Still clutching the pen, I raced for the stairs, out of my mind with fear. All the times my mother told me I needed to get a landline phone installed haunted me in that moment. My only means of calling for help was upstairs, beside my bed, in the form of my smart phone.

She was never going to let me hear the end of this.

If I survive. The thought floated through my head like a vicious taunt. Another light scuffling sound upstairs had my heart thumping even harder.

My God, it might not be me they hurt!

I wasn't quiet on my way up the old wooden steps. In fact, I sounded like a herd of elephants that needed to lose about twenty pounds.

Good.

It would draw all the attention of the no good dirty rotten bastards in here.

Come get me, assholes.

It was dark upstairs except for the nightlight that lit up the hallway. Against the long wall across from that light, I saw a dark, lurking shadow pass. I gasped and my blood pressure skyrocketed so high that my scalp likely should have blown off the top of my head.

Holy shit, this was scary.

But I had to be strong. I had to be a fighter. I *was* a fighter.

The intruder appeared at the top of the stairs, slipping out of my bedroom just as I cleared the top step. His body tensed when he saw me, and then he rushed me without warning.

Not knowing what else to do, I used the pen as a weapon, striking out and using the force with which he threw himself at me to impale him with the writing instrument.

He grunted in pain.

Score!

Clearly, I was terrible at sports because stabbing a man twice your size who had broken into your home with an itty bitty pen wasn't enough to swing the game in your favor.

All it did was piss him off.

He straightened and yanked the pen out of him, looked at it, then looked at me.

He was wearing one of those black ski masks that frankly scared the bejeezus out of me. I threw my arms out to shove past him to run back along the hallway, but that was a bad idea, too.

He caught me, wrapped his meaty, vise-like fingers around my forearms, and swung me around. I slammed into the wall, my head bouncing off like a child's ball.

Darkness closed in around the edges of my vision, and I fought it like a little hellcat. I would not pass out. I couldn't. He depended on me.

"No," I whispered, my head exploding with pain.

The man advancing on me laughed low. It made my skin crawl.

Another man appeared behind him. He was just as big as his friend.

"You're going to pay for that, bitch." The man closest to me promised.

Before I could do anything, he fisted a hand in my hair and dragged me down the stairs.

2

The only light on downstairs was the small one above the stove in the kitchen. While I couldn't see the intruders that clearly because of their masks and the crappy lighting in here, I was pretty glad they couldn't see me that well either.

I didn't want them to see my fear.

The minute someone sensed your fear, things got worse.

After a rough trip down the stairs (I was going to be covered in bruises), I was dragged into the kitchen and shoved at one of the two chairs at the little bistro set in the corner.

"Sit down," he growled.

Sitting wasn't really an option with the way he shoved me. I stumbled and fell, the top of my forehead colliding with one of the black wrought iron chairs. I landed on my hands and knees, willing myself to shake off the pain.

Get up, Elle. Get up.

I slapped a palm onto the seat of the chair and hoisted myself up to sit down. I thought longingly of my cell phone, which still was upstairs. I should have listened to my mother.

If I survived this, I was sooo getting a landline. And one of those life alert thingies for old people. And a gun.

Yeah, definitely a gun.

"What do you want?" I asked, dabbing at my forehead that was now bleeding.

Intruder number one dropped the bloody pen on my island—*gross*—and applied pressure to the hole I gave him in his side.

"We just wanted to talk all nice like," he said with one of those Jersey accents. "But you didn't greet us very nice like."

"If you wanted polite, you should have rang the doorbell," I snapped.

Intruder number two chuckled from the other side of the island. "She's a spicy one."

"Shut it," intruder one growled. He was wearing a black ski mask, and in the dim lighting I could see that his partner was wearing a blue one.

Both men were wearing black jeans and black jackets. I mean, really, I know they were invading my home and all, but they could have dressed better.

After yelling at Blue Mask, he pulled his hand away from his middle and I saw it was covered in red. I got some sick satisfaction out of that. In fact, it made me feel a little stronger, like I could fight my way out of this.

"You need a Band-Aid boss?" Blue Mask said. Clearly, he wasn't the sharpest crayon in the box.

I couldn't help it. I snickered.

Black Mask's shoulders tightened and his eyes swung up to mine. He stared at me for a long, hard second. I got this twisty feeling in my stomach. I shouldn't have laughed. I'd made him angry.

"Yeah," he said, not a hint of anger in his tone. "Can you find me a Band-Aid?"

"Sure thing, boss," Blue Mask said and headed for the stairs.

Panic rose in me again. I didn't want him up there, but I knew there wasn't a way to stop him. "Hey," I said.

He looked at me.

"The first aid kit is under the bathroom sink. First door on the left."

"Thanks," he said like we were friends and this wasn't some weird hostage situation. As soon as he left the room, the man in the black mask backhanded me across the face.

I gasped, my head rotating sharply on my shoulders because of the unexpected strike. The pungent taste of blood covered my tongue when I swallowed. My tooth must have cut into the inside of my lip when he hit me.

I stared up at him, lifting my chin.

"You won't be laughing when I'm finished with you."

The adrenaline in my system was starting to die down a bit and I began to shake. Fear crept into my fighter's attitude.

"Why are you here?" I asked, knowing he wanted more than conversation.

My eyes slid over to my hot tea. Steam was still rising slowly off the top. It seemed like forever since I poured that water. Clearly it had been merely minutes.

Above us, I heard the man in the bathroom. He wasn't being delicate as he looked for the kit. I knew when I went up there, my bathroom was going to be trashed. I winced at all the noise he was making and bit my lip to hold back a broken sob.

"You're a personal chef, right?"

"Yes," I replied, still listening to the ruckus upstairs.

"You work at the White House."

"Yes," I said again, distracted. Another loud thump carried to my ears. Geez, how hard was it to reach under the cabinet and pull out the first aid kit?

And then the sound I was dreading most cut through the night. It also cut through my heart. My very bad situation just got worse.

The sound of my crying son, Jack, floated down the steps.

My eyes shot to the man in the black mask. I saw his lips curve into a sadistic smile.

"Please," I whispered, my voice hoarse. "I'll do anything you want. Just don't hurt him."

"What kind of man do you take me for?" he said, but we both knew what kind of man he was.

"Please," I said again. I wasn't above begging. It was my son. He was my entire life.

Jack's crying grew louder, and my stomach tied itself into knots. He was probably wondering where I was, why I wasn't coming. He probably heard all the noise and was scared to death. Unable to take the torturous thoughts, I leapt out of my chair and ran toward the door.

Asshole was right there, grabbing me back and tossing me into the teetering chair. "You do what I say and no one will get hurt."

I didn't believe him, but God help me, I wanted to.

I swallowed down the sob stretching out my

windpipe.

Jack's crying abruptly stopped, and I began to panic. "Just let me go check on him," I entreated.

He laughed. "Maybe wondering what the hell is going on up there with my partner and your kid will make you more agreeable."

"Just tell me what you want!" I shouted, tears pricking the backs of my eyes.

I judged the distance between the man and the door, considering my chances of running for it.

"Don't even think about it, bitch," he said, reading my thoughts.

Tears rolled down my cheeks and I wiped them away quickly. When I pulled my hand back, I noticed there was some blood mixed in. I dabbed at my forehead again, noting it was still bleeding, trickling down the side of my face.

"You didn't answer me," he said like he didn't notice or care I was totally freaking out. "Do you work as the president's personal chef or not?"

He didn't ask me that before. Did he? How the hell did he know where I worked? A very bad feeling crawled over me.

"Yes," I answered, still thinking of Jack.

"You cook his meals?"

"For the staff and the first family," I answered, skirting the question.

He backhanded me again. "Yes or no?"

I swallowed, keeping my head down. "Yes."

"Good."

The silence upstairs was too much. I got up and sprinted past the intruder, skirting around his grabby hands and toward the stairs. "Jack!" I called, unable to keep the panic from my voice, but not caring. I didn't want my son to be scared, but maybe if he heard my worry, he would cry out.

Movement at the top of the stairs grabbed my attention and my steps slowed just a fraction. It was my mistake. Black mask tackled me from behind. I went down at the bottom of the stairs, my body hitting the floor like it was an anchor falling to the base of the sea. He wasn't gentle, and I think he enjoyed the sick sound my bones made when I hit.

He grabbed the back of my head, yanking the long strands of my hair and forcing my head back. His teeth purposely grazed the side of my ear when he said, "You keep this up and you're going to regret it."

I struggled beneath him, wanting desperately to get to Jack.

"Seems she wants the kid," Black mask yelled upstairs. "Toss him down here."

"No!" I screamed, struggling anew. "No." I managed to get one hand free and reached behind me to claw at his face.

He grunted as my nails just grazed his skin.

"Do it," he roared.

I looked up at the top of the stairs where the man in the blue mask was holding Jack in his arms. Jack was staring down at me with wide eyes as I screamed.

"It's okay, baby," I tried to tell him. I was a horrible liar, my words not convincing at all.

"I don't hurt kids," the man holding Jack said.

I whimpered in relief. "Thank you," I cried.

"You fucking moron!" Black Mask yelled.

"You shouldn't cuss in front of them either," he said as he carried Jack down the stairs.

I struggled and was wrenched up off the floor. Next to me, Jack held out his little chubby arms for me to take him. I reached for him but was jerked away, bouncing into the wall.

"No," was all my captor said.

Jack started to cry.

So did I.

The man with the blue mask frowned. "No need to be such an asshole, boss."

He stepped between me and "the boss" and handed Jack out. I snatched him away, cradling him against my chest. Jack pushed his little face into the side of my neck and the scent of his shampoo wrapped around my senses. Another sob ripped from my throat.

"Come on," Blue Mask said and led me into the kitchen.

I didn't go back to the table. I wasn't sitting down. It made me feel vulnerable. Instead, I put the island between us, my mind spinning with ways to get the hell out of here. Now that I had Jack, I could think more clearly.

"We know everything about you, Elle Bond," the man in the blue mask said, drawing my attention.

"We know you get up every morning at five a.m. and spend an hour with your kid here before you take him over to your mother's house so she can watch him for the day. We know where your mother lives. We know she lives alone, just like you and the kid. We know the route you drive to work, the route you take home. We know the coffee shop on the corner you go to every morning just after six. We know you leave work at eleven and go to your mother's to see your kid before heading back to work to make dinner."

The more he talked about my routine, the more terrified I became. He knew everything. *Everything.* They'd been watching me for weeks, and I hadn't even realized. How could I just go about my normal routine—how could I just live my life and not realize people were watching me?

What kind of mother was I to not know that her son was in danger?

"I don't understand," I said, my voice shaky. Jack made a little sound and I tucked him closer to me.

"We have a job for you, Ms. Bond," Blue Mask said.

"I have a job."

"What he meant to say was you're going to do something for us and you don't have a choice," Black Mask replied, his voice hard.

"What?" A fearful knot blocked my esophagus.

"We want you to kill the president."

I blinked.

Then I blinked again.

Surely I heard them wrong. There was no way on God's green earth that two men just broke into my apartment to order me to kill the president of the United States.

They stood there staring at me like they were deadly serious.

Overwhelmed, I started to laugh. This was ridiculous. "Who put you up to this?" I asked, thinking surely this was some kind of joke gone wrong.

Black Mask didn't say a word, but he did reach into that ugly black jacket and pull out a dark vial with a dropper lid. He sat it on the counter. "This is very potent poison. Completely untraceable in the bloodstream."

I stared at the vial.

"You have access to the president's meals, his food. Just a couple drops will kill him."

Oh. My. God. They were serious.

"I'm not going to the kill the president!" I burst out.

"You will, Ms. Bond," Blue Mask said gravely.

"No." I shook my head. This was unbelievable. "Who are you?" I demanded.

"It doesn't matter who we are. Do what we say or you'll regret it."

"What?" I said. "You'll kill me if I don't poison the president?" I snorted. This was stupid.

"No," said Black Mask. "We won't kill you. We'll kill *him*."

His eyes went to Jack. I sucked in a breath. They were threatening my son.

"You would kill an innocent baby?" I whispered.

"Oh, yes. And then we'll come for your mother. We will destroy everything in your life until it's just you, all alone."

"I'll call the police," I replied bravely.

They laughed. They actually chuckled like it was funny. "We *own* the police force."

"You can't possibly…"

"You have no idea who we work for. The police can't help you. Go ahead. Call them. We'll make sure you're the one who goes down for plotting to kill the commander in chief. What will happen to your son then?"

I recoiled from their words. My knees were shaking and I felt like I might fall over at any time. I was lightheaded. My face hurt. My body hurt. I had blood running in my eye, blurring my vision even further. My son was in the presence of killers, and I was being told the police wouldn't and couldn't help me.

"And if I do it?" I asked. I had no intention of

killing the president. None at all. I was not a murderer. I could barely kill a spider without feeling guilty. But I had to ask. I had to know. And I wanted them to think I was considering this.

"Your son gets to live."

"What about me?" I asked.

"As long as you keep your mouth shut, you will, too."

I didn't believe them. There was no way in hell that they would let me live, even if I did it. They would want to erase all loose ends.

I swallowed. I didn't know what to say. I wanted them to go. "I'll think about it."

Black Mask grunted. "You don't have a choice. Do it. Do it soon. If you don't, we'll be back, and next time we won't be as nice." He went to the back door and turned the lock. After another hard glance at me, he disappeared into the dark.

My eyes swung to Blue Mask. He walked toward the door, but instead of going outside, he changed course and stopped right in front of me. "Do what he says," he whispered. "Just do it. I don't want to hurt that boy, but he'll make me. Just do it."

He left, closing the door quietly behind him.

My knees gave out, and I slid down the cabinets until I was sitting on the tile floor. I felt totally numb. Almost like I was living in some bad dream and just needed to wake up. But this wasn't a dream because I had yet to fall asleep tonight.

Jack sat up in my lap, straddling my waist, and looked at me. I brushed a thumb across his creamy, chubby cheek. Fear seized my throat at just the suggestion that something horrible could happen to him.

He gave me a toothless grin and then yawned.

I suppressed the ugly cry.

I pushed myself up off the kitchen floor to go rock Jack back to sleep. At barely two years old, I doubted what happened tonight would be enough to keep him from drifting back off to dream land.

But me?

I wondered if I would ever sleep again.

3

After I put Jack to bed, I checked all the doors and windows, making sure they were locked. Then I stared at my phone for a long time, debating if I should call the police. I was so confused. I didn't know what to believe, but I was scared enough that it kept me from dialing.

I decided to try and calm down, to really try and think before I did anything. So I went into the bathroom to see what kind of damage was waiting for me. Of course the place was a mess. I spent over an hour cleaning it up and throwing out the broken items. The first aid kit was strewn all over the floor, and it took forever to gather it all up and dump it back into the kit. I wasn't about to organize it all.

When that was done, I looked in the mirror and recoiled immediately. I'd forgotten about the cut on my forehead. I lifted up the sticky long strands of blond hair and saw the neat gash near my hairline.

It was no longer bleeding, having clotted over. It was red and irritated, of course, but didn't appear to be so deep it needed stitches. I had dried blood on my face, and my lower lip was slightly swollen from where I assumed I cut it on my tooth. My cheek was red from where he hit me, but it appeared I wouldn't have a noticeable bruise.

I cleaned up my face, washing it gently with cool water and a little soap. When I was done, I put on some moisturizer and then cleaned the cut lightly. I didn't want to reopen it, but I was afraid it would get all nasty if I didn't do anything.

After applying peroxide, it was bleeding again but only lightly. So I applied a little antiseptic and then put a small butterfly bandage over it. Thankfully, it was so close to my hairline that I would be able to fix my hair so it wasn't visible.

I brushed out my hair and changed into a fresh pair of pajamas. I had taken a shower just before the men burst in, but I felt dirty and wanted something unsullied to wear.

I checked on Jack for like the millionth time and stood over his crib to watch him sleep. It was my job to protect him. I was all he had. Having a son and being a single mother wasn't easy. Thank God for my mother or I didn't know where I'd be. But even still, I couldn't imagine not having Jack. I loved him more than anything.

And now he was being threatened.

It would have been easier if they'd threatened to kill me.

Clearly, they knew my weak spot. Whoever the hell they were. I believed they knew all about me. Some of the information he knew was too personal. It worried me. Who were these people? I didn't know, but something told me they weren't just two guys who sat in their basement and made up this elaborate plot in the spur of the moment.

This had been thought out. Planned.

What the hell was I going to do?

I couldn't do it. Maybe calling their bluff and going to the cops was the best thing to do. Surely they couldn't have the *entire* police force in Washington D.C. in their pocket. And besides, even if they did, if I went in there talking about conspiracy theories to kill the president, someone would listen.

Wouldn't they?

We'll make sure you're the one who goes down for plotting to kill the commander in chief.

I shivered.

Leaving Jack's room, I clutched my phone and went down to the kitchen. I turned on all the lights and rechecked all the doors. My tea had finally gone cold, and I poured it down the sink.

The poison sitting in the dark vial taunted me. It made me sick. I couldn't even lie to myself and pretend this was just a dream. The proof was sitting right there.

What if it wasn't really poison? What if this was some elaborate hoax. On impulse, I snatched the stuff off the counter and untwisted the lid. I was afraid to smell it, to get too close to the liquid. If it really was poison, I didn't want to be its first victim.

Instead, I filled the little dropper and dispensed it on a little pot of green ivy trailing down the windowsill toward the sink.

Nothing happened.

I recapped the stuff and hid it on the very top shelf of a cabinet I never used. I left all the lights on downstairs and wearily climbed back up the steps. In Jack's room, I sat in the rocker and covered my legs with a soft blanket.

In a few hours, I was supposed to be going into work. How was I supposed to just go about like nothing happened? I couldn't. I was going to have to go to the police.

Or better yet, I would go to work and I would tell someone there. They would believe me. I worked there; they knew me. They would trust what I said. I could show them the cut on my head and the bruises marring my skin.

An image of Spencer swam before my heavy eyes and my lids drifted closed. For some reason, thinking about Spence made everything seem a little less terrifying. I clung to the thought of his honey-colored eyes and the way they crinkled at the corners when he was sneaking cookies from the kitchen.

It didn't take long for sheer exhaustion to pull me under, and I fell into sleep, an unwilling captor of fatigue.

It felt like I was barely asleep for ten minutes when something woke me. I jerked awake immediately, a little disoriented, until I remembered I was in Jack's room. My brain was foggy from sleep. My eyes felt as if they had one hundred pounds of sand in them, and my entire body ached like a giant bruise.

And then I remembered why I was sleeping in Jack's room and not mine.

The fog in my brain blew away, and I sat up, ignoring the protests of my limbs. The light between the blinds was dim. The sun would be coming up soon. It was probably my internal alarm clock that woke me.

I went over to Jack's crib, smiling a little because I knew I would see his little angelic face, and leaned over the railing.

My entire body jerked.

The crib was empty.

I did a double take, thinking I was still half asleep.

I wasn't.

Jack was gone.

"Jack!" I called as pure terror pounded through my veins. My vision blurred and my body swayed, threatening to pass out. I didn't have time to pass out.

How in the hell did this happen? I'd been in here all night!

"Calm down, Elle," I told myself. "Maybe he finally learned how to climb out."

I raced from the room, checking the bathroom, my bedroom, and the small hall closet. No sign of him. My heart began to hammer against my ribs as I approached the steps. I was beyond petrified I would see his little body lying at the bottom of the steps.

He wasn't there either.

"Jack!" I called for him again, praying to God he would make some sort of sound. I'd give anything to hear a "Momma" right about now.

It was achingly silent. I raced through the house, tearing it apart, looking in every possible spot he could be. He wasn't there.

Jack wasn't there.

Someone kidnapped my son.

I was practically hyperventilating when I grabbed my keys and phone and raced outside to my car. I was going to the police station immediately. I needed as much help as I could get.

Where was he? Was he okay? Was he confused? Was he hungry, crying? How in the hell could someone just walk in and take him from literally right beneath my nose?

The car door slammed behind me and I fought my shaking hands, trying to get the damn key into the ignition. I was sobbing openly, horrible sounds of pain ripping from my lungs.

"Momma," said a little voice from behind me.

I spun around so fast it hurt my head. "Jack!" I cried.

He was sitting in his car seat, still wearing the little pajamas I'd dressed him in the night before. I catapulted out of the car and rushed around to the back door and wrenched it open. I pulled Jack into my arms and cried, utterly relieved he was okay.

"Mommy was so scared," I told him, kissing the top of his dark head. "What happened to you?" I asked, pulling him back slightly so I could look him over for injury.

He appeared to be fine. Not a single mark on him, and he wasn't crying so I figured that was good.

I hugged him again, so tight he squealed, and I pulled him back again with a smile. I heard the crinkling of paper and wrinkled my nose. That was an odd sound. I grabbed my keys and went back inside, still clutching Jack.

I heard the sound again and looked down at his onesie. It seemed like the paper was inside his pajamas.

I laid him on the couch and reached inside, pulling out a crumpled piece of paper.

Next time he won't be so easy to find.

I ran into the bathroom and threw up.

What in the hell was I going to do?

4

Some days going to work was hard. I felt guilty a lot for dropping Jack off with my mom and leaving. I felt like I was missing moments with him that I would regret later. I wondered when he grew up if he would have more memories with his grandma than he did with me.

I wondered if I was a good enough mother. I wondered if it made me a bad person for loving what I did and wanting to do it.

But today, going to work was hard for a completely different reason.

I wondered what would happen if I wasn't there to protect him. I worried that something horrible would happen to Jack or my mom. Before leaving, I gave Mom a wad of cash and told her to take Jack to the zoo. I didn't know if sending her out in public was a good idea or not. I wasn't sure if the crowd at the zoo would be a good thing or a bad thing. But it made me feel a fraction better that they would be with a ton of other people instead of alone at my mom's place.

She noticed how tired I looked. She told me I was white as a ghost. I lied and told her I had an upset stomach. She believed me.

I drove to work with sweaty palms, checking my rearview mirror every three seconds. After going through security and making my way to my parking spot, I sat in the car for a few minutes, getting ready to turn on my fake smile.

I knew I needed to do something, to tell someone, but this morning left me completely shaken. They took Jack and I didn't even know it. Yeah, he wasn't hurt. *This time*. Could I take a chance like that again?

In the kitchen, I made it a point to work off by myself. First, I busied myself in the small kitchen office, planning out the menu for a dinner that was taking place next week. Yeah, I usually had this done by now, but it was a last-minute thing and I wanted something special. Once I was satisfied with the menu, I handed it off to one of the other kitchen staff and asked them to put in the grocery order so we would have everything we needed for it.

Then I decided to make some bread. It was a long process, it was a quiet process, and I figured the rhythm of kneading the dough might help me relax.

The bustle of the kitchen usually excited me, made me feel like I was part of a team. Today, I found the noise disturbing and all the people suffocating. All I wanted to do was go home.

I was thinking about my options, trying to get over the shock of everything that happened since the night before, when a familiar form appeared in the doorway of the little room where I was making the bread.

I looked up from the task to see Spencer leaning against the doorjamb, his shoulders nearly filling the doorway. His hair was slightly mussed and he had a cookie in both hands.

"I think you were the Cookie Monster in a previous life," I joked, though the playfulness just wasn't there in my tone.

He popped an entire one in his mouth and chewed. "I wouldn't look good with blue hair."

That got a small smile, but it disappeared quickly. Just the mere idea of smiling at a time like this felt so wrong.

"Making bread?" he asked.

"Yep," I replied.

He pushed out of the doorway and waltzed into the room. The black suit he wore was completely wrinkle free. I knew he had a gun on his person somewhere. Maybe I should get a gun. When the men came back, I could just shoot them. It would be self-defense. Right?

"Earth to Elle," Spencer said, stopping on the other side of the island.

I looked up.

"What's wrong with you?" he asked, blunt.

"Nothing."

He finished off the last cookie and brushed his hands off over the floor. "You're lying."

"Am not," I said, kneading the dough some more and using it as an excuse not to look at him.

"You're white as a ghost, your hands are shaking like a leaf," he pointed out, "and you're not staring at me with those bedroom eyes of yours."

I jerked up. "Bedroom eyes?" I felt my eyebrow rise.

He grinned.

"I'm fine," I said, returning to the bread. "Just having an off day, I guess."

I felt his stare as I worked. He didn't say anything. Usually by now he'd be gone. He'd come in, steal cookies, make a couple ornery comments, then disappear. I looked forward to those moments. It made me angry I couldn't enjoy it today.

A sharp sound of something hitting the ground followed immediately by shattering glass made me jump. Adrenaline surged through my bloodstream, and I pressed a hand to my chest as I looked around for the cause of the disruption.

My eyes sought out every corner of the little kitchen, searching for some sign of attack. Had the men gotten in here somehow? Were they coming for me?

What about Jack?

Panic pretty much took over my entire body. Even though the room was empty, I still wasn't able to gain control of my emotions. I backed up, skirting across the floor until my back came up against the nearby wall.

The bread dough lay on the island, forgotten.

Through the clutches of the panic attack, I saw Spencer's mouth moving, but I couldn't hear the words. I knew I needed to respond, but I couldn't. I just couldn't.

Spencer leapt over the island like it wasn't even an obstacle, his feet landing on the ground aptly. He rushed across the room, his face a mask of concern and concentration. His body approached mine as I plastered myself against the wall, desperately trying to breathe.

At first, I worried the way he crowded my space would make me panic worse, would make me feel like I was being cornered. But Spencer didn't scare me. His large hand wrapped around the back of my neck and applied gentle pressure to the muscles that were completely locked up.

"Breathe in," he said, his voice totally calm and reasonable.

It was that tone that seemed to break through the worst of my panic. With another squeeze to the back of my neck, I opened my mouth and air rushed in.

My body sagged against the wall, but Spencer kept hold of the back of my neck, still kneading the muscles.

He angled his body so he was directly in front of me. The only thing I could see was him and the broad width of his shoulders. He smelled good; his cologne, slightly musky, seeped into the edges of my senses, bringing with it even more calm.

Spencer was basically a professional bodyguard. He was totally calm right now. If something bad was happening, he would be reacting. He would be doing something. Clearly, I was safe. Clearly, he would make sure of it.

A few more minutes of even breathing and his scent so close and my body released its death grip it had over me. A fine sheen of sweat broke out over my skin, and I leaned against the wall because my knees felt incredibly weak.

When I was okay enough to speak, embarrassment washed over me. I looked up at Spencer. "I'm really sorry."

"What are you sorry for, darlin'?"

He had a deep voice. A soothing voice. If he were a singer, he would for sure be an alto.

"I panicked," I said as if it hadn't been totally obvious.

He loosened his grip on the back of my neck but didn't release me. I was glad for that. His touch was grounding, and frankly, it gave me somewhere to focus other than the horrible thoughts forcing their way into my mind.

"Someone out in the main kitchen dropped something," he said. "It broke."

I nodded. "I guess I'm a little jumpy today." I tried to give him a sheepish smile. I have no clue if I succeeded.

He was frowning when I stole a glance at him. His honey eyes captured mine, refusing to let go. I felt the way he searched my gaze, like he was able to extract all the info he wanted without asking a single question.

"What happened?" he whispered, shifting so he was just a little bit closer.

"Nothing." I lied.

"You just had a panic attack. You look like hell."

I made a scoffing sound and laughed. "Gee, way to make a girl feel good," I said, tilting my head back against the wall and looking up at the ceiling. I kept my head back a little because tears were threatening to spill over and I wanted to keep them under control.

A change came over Spencer. His body became still and in that stillness, he emanated great tension. His hand withdrew from my neck and he lifted it, brushing at the side-swept bangs I styled myself with this morning.

"What happened to your head?" he said, his fingertips brushing over the butterfly bandage.

I winced. Of all the people to notice it.

"Just an accident," I said, ducking my head so my hair fell over it. It was bruising around the cut this morning and still very sore.

He grabbed my chin and tilted my face up so he could scrutinize it. "Your lower lip is swollen," he noted, his eyes narrowing into angry slits.

Without any notice, he grasped my bottom lip and pulled it out, rudely poking around on the inside.

"Hey," I protested, my voice sounding funny because he was holding my face hostage.

"There's a cut inside your lip," he growled.

I jerked my face away and tried to slip around him, to get away from the close inspection. Spencer grabbed my upper arm and I yelped. Then I stiffened, pissed at myself for giving away yet another injury.

Slowly, deliberately, he withdrew his hand from my arm. I moved to rush away. He wasn't about to allow it. Instead of grabbing me again, he wrapped his wide, solid arm around my waist, pulling me so my side was flush against his chest.

My stomach did little summersaults. I'd often wondered what it would be like to be in his arms. Even feeling scared out of my mind and trying to get away from him wasn't enough to keep me from realizing that if felt damned amazing.

"Show me," he murmured.

"No."

"I will rip that top right off your body, Elle," he warned.

I looked up at him. "Please, Spencer."

"I know the look of a wounded bird," he whispered. "You don't look wounded, darlin'. You look downright beaten." The southern twang in his tone took away any kind of sting I might have felt at his honest words.

I slumped against him with a shaky breath releasing from within me.

His arm tightened, supporting me, and for several long moments, I let him hold me. I let his strength wrap around me, and I let myself believe that everything would be okay. Hell, being in his arms like this, I almost thought it was true.

"You can talk to me," he murmured.

I pulled away and stood there debating. It didn't take long because the truth was holding all this inside was too hard. I felt like the glass out in the kitchen, ready to shatter at any moment. I didn't have anyone to talk to. I felt alone and scared. Spencer was the closest person I had as a friend.

Yes, I realize how utterly sad that made me.

I was wearing a white button-up shirt. It was pretty standard and professional-looking. The sleeves were rolled just slightly so they didn't get messy while making the bread. Normally, I would have them all the way to my elbows, but not today. I had bruises on my forearms.

Silently, I unbuttoned the shirt all the way down to my navel. I was dressed in a white tank top beneath my shirt so nothing of my body was overly exposed.

Once again, Spencer shifted, blocking me with his body so if someone happened to walk in, they wouldn't see my state of undress. They would only get treated to the view of his broad back.

Without hesitation, I slid the shirt down, revealing my shoulder, upper arm, and back. He sucked in a breath between his lips. I didn't bother to look down at the purple marks marring my skin. I already knew what they looked like and how they got there. I didn't need to see them to relive the memory.

"Who did this to you?" Spencer said, his voice hard and cold.

I slid my shirt back up and worked on the buttons, unsure where to begin with my answer.

"Elle," he said, reaching out to touch me, but he stopped. His hand hovered just above me, like he wasn't sure where he should touch.

"I'm scared, Spence," I admitted, my voice shaking. "I don't know what to do."

The muscles in his jaw locked up, protruding out the corners of his face. He looked angular and, frankly, a little mean.

"You tell me. I'll make this right." His voice was so sincere that I believed him.

"I don't think you can."

His hovering hand settled, wrapping once more around the back of my neck. Perhaps he thought that was a safe zone because he could see I wasn't bruised there.

Or maybe he knew touching me there felt so damn good.

"I damn well will," he vowed.

Some laughter drifted in from outside the door, and I glanced at the forgotten blob of dough on the counter beside us. "This really isn't a good place to talk," I said.

He made a frustrated sound.

"Can we talk after work?" I asked tentatively. I didn't really know what his personal life was like. I had no idea if he had other obligations.

His shoulders relaxed a little. "Yeah. Of course we can."

"I don't know what time you get off," I said, moving away from him. I loved his close proximity, but I couldn't allow myself to lean on him too much. I needed to stand on my own two feet. "I actually don't know much about you," I added.

"Not much to tell," he said.

"You must work long hours." I moved back toward the bread, hoping the dough hadn't begun to dry out already. I picked it up and flipped it over to knead it some more. It seemed like Spencer was always here. Here when I got here, and I'd seen him a couple times as I was leaving the building when my day was over.

"I'll be available when you get off."

I pounded the dough and a wave of dizziness came over me. I swayed on my feet.

"Whoa," he said, reaching out to steady me.

Marla, the kitchen manager, appeared in the doorway.

"Elle?" she asked. "Is everything okay?"

"She's not feeling well," Spencer answered for me. "I think she needs to go home."

Marla came farther into the room, her eagle-eyed gaze taking in my face. "You certainly don't look like you feel well."

"I'm sorry," I said, not wanting to inconvenience the staff. "I'll be fine." The last thing I needed was to lose this job. I'd work so hard and sacrificed so much to get here.

She waved her hand. "You've never missed a day since you started here. Go home. Rest."

"But the first family will need dinner tonight." I protested.

"And they will get it. But if you are ill, you shouldn't be preparing their food anyway."

I wanted to tell her what was making me sick wasn't contagious, but I didn't want to explain.

"I already gave Mark the completed menu for next week's dinner party. He's ordering the items we need this afternoon."

"I have every confidence that you missing half a day of work will not mess up your tightly run kitchen in the least. Now go on home." She pointed to the door with her thumb.

I wiped my hands on a nearby white towel. Relief chased away the worst of my anxiety. At least this way I could see Jack and be with him all day. I would know he was safe. "Thank you."

"If you're still ill tomorrow, call in and let me know."

"I will." I promised.

Marla turned her attention to Spencer and a twinkle came into her eye. "Down here stealing cookies again, are you?"

He grinned, a dimple on either side of his lips. "Gotta have my sugar."

Marla chuckled. "I think I'll send an entire tin upstairs with you. That way all the others can have some sugar, too."

"Yes, ma'am," he drawled.

"There you go with that southern charm," she called on her way to presumably get a tin full of cookies.

She'd forgotten I was here already. I didn't blame her. Spencer had a way of taking all the attention in a room.

I pulled off my apron and hung it on a hook, then went to get someone to come and finish the bread I was making. The back of my neck prickled a little as I felt his stare, but he didn't say a word, and for that I was grateful.

I'd left my bag in the small office this morning and when I came out with it draped over my shoulder, I was surprised to see Spencer lounging against the wall, holding the tin.

"What are you doing?" I asked.

"We're supposed to talk."

"I said not here."

He pushed off the wall. I couldn't help but notice the way the black jacket of his suit hugged his shoulders.

"I'll drive you home."

"No," I said quickly.

His eyes narrowed.

I couldn't let him do that. What if those men were still watching? They might suspect that I told someone. They could take it out on Jack.

"I can drive myself."

"You almost passed out," he pointed out.

"I'm fine," I growled.

"Down, girl," he said, giving me a grin. Then he walked off down the hall. "I'll meet you outside."

I stared after him. Did he think I was just going to listen? Maybe he was used to women doing what he wanted. I might be charmed by him, I might think he was totally hot, but I wasn't about to do as I was told.

As he went another member of the staff came around the corner and stopped when he saw Spencer. He was dressed in an identical suit so I knew he was also part of the Secret Service. "Spencer, did you forget about the meeting?" the man said.

Spencer's back stiffened. I heard a low curse. "Yeah, sorry I'm late."

The man shook his head and looked down the hall at me. I felt my cheeks heat because I basically got caught eavesdropping.

Spencer followed the man's eyes and glanced at me. Then he looked back at his co-worker. "Can you fill me in later? I need to be somewhere."

"Yeah you need to be at the meeting. The security at that dinner next week is a big job."

Spencer sighed.

"It's okay," I called out, not wanting him to feel torn. I wasn't his responsibility anyway. "We can talk later."

I didn't wait around for him to argue. Instead, I hurried around the corner and went outside to the parking lot, dialing my mother's cell phone. She answered on the second ring. "Elle? Is everything okay?"

I could hear a lot of noise in the background. "Hi, Mom. Are you and Jack at the zoo?"

"Yes, he's having a great time."

I smiled. He loved the zoo. His little eyes always lit up when he saw the animals. "That's great." I cleared my throat. "My stomach isn't feeling any better so I'm coming home. It's better I don't work with the food today."

"I can leave right now and meet you."

"No," I said quickly. I wanted her to be there in the crowd for a little longer. "Don't rush. Jack loves that place. I'm just going to lie down anyway."

"I'll bring him home afterward," she said, relenting.

"Sounds great," I said, fishing my car keys out of my pocket. I disconnected the call and dumped the phone into the twilight zone that was my bag.

My head was muddled with thoughts and fears as I hit the unlock button on the wireless remote and reached for the door handle of the driver's side.

But that's as far as I made it.

A large hand grabbed me from behind.

5

I screamed and the keys in my hand hit the pavement with a loud clatter.

"Shit," Spencer muttered, letting go of me immediately. "I didn't mean to scare you."

I swung around, feeling like I'd just run fifteen miles. "Yeah? Well, you did."

His lips drew into a line and he shoved a hand through his hair. "What the hell is going on, Elle?" he demanded.

"I thought you had a meeting?" I questioned.

"I told you to wait for me," he countered.

"Does everyone do what you tell them to?" I crossed my arms over my chest.

"If they know what's good for them."

I snorted.

He bent down and snatched the keys off the pavement before I could even blink. "Hey!" I protested, reaching for them.

"I'm driving."

"I'm pretty sure you were just told in there you had to stay?" I questioned again.

"You're more important right now," he said softly.

My stomach did a little flip. It seemed appropriate his eyes were the color of honey, because his words were just as smooth.

"I don't want anyone to see us together," I said truthfully.

Clearly, I was not as smooth as he was.

He rubbed a hand over his jaw. "That's the first time a woman's ever said that to me."

I rolled my eyes and suppressed a laugh. "I don't think your big ego will fit in my car anyway."

He pretended he didn't hear my very good insult and tucked my keys into the pocket of his black dress pants. He was wearing a pair of wraparound shades, but even with his eyes covered, I could still feel their amber gaze.

"Come on," he said, gesturing with his head to the other side of the lot. "I'll drive."

I followed, not because I wanted to, but because he had my keys.

Okay, maybe it was because I wanted to.

He had his hands tucked into the pockets of his slacks and the action pulled the fabric taut across his tight ass. I couldn't help but stare at it as I trailed along behind him.

Please, you totally would be looking, too.

"Are you staring at my ass?" he asked over his shoulder.

"No," I said like I was completely disgusted by the suggestion.

Thank God he couldn't see the mortification in my eyes.

His chuckle floated back to me, and I wanted to die from embarrassment.

We stopped beside a black Mustang without a speck of dirt on it. "I should have known this was your car," I said.

He grinned. "She drew your eye, eh?"

"I suppose so," I admitted. I did tend to give it a look when I walked through the lot every day.

"Let me tell ya something," he drawled. "You can tell a lot about man from his car."

"Is that so?" I said, amused.

He crossed his arms over his chest and leaned against the side of the shiny black paint and nodded.

"And what does this car say about you?" I asked.

He grinned. "That just like this car, I'm American-made and full of horsepower."

I laughed even as the excitement in my blood skyrocketed.

"Come on," he said, giving me another of his heart-stopping grins, and pulled open the passenger-side door. I slid in without a second thought.

The interior was gray leather and it was just as spotless as the outside. It smelled like him in here, musky and deep. It wasn't an overpowering scent, though. It was relaxed. I liked it.

Hell, I liked everything about Spencer.

Before he climbed in, the black jacket he was wearing flew past my face and landed in the backseat. Then he folded himself into the driver's seat, his long legs eating up most of the floor space. He started up the engine and adjusted the vents so cool air blew over me and then proceeded to roll up his sleeves to his elbows. He had strong-looking forearms.

"Ready?" he said when he was done, looking across the closed-in space.

I nodded.

He drove like he'd been doing it his entire life. He was completely comfortable behind the wheel, navigating the traffic-laden streets of downtown D.C. with barely any effort at all.

"Where do you live?" he asked.

My stomach twisted at the thought of my townhouse. It just didn't feel like a safe place anymore. It felt like somewhere I was caged and on display, somewhere that unseemly people could watch me.

"I don't want to go there."

I felt his eyes slide over to me, but he didn't say anything else. A few minutes later, he said, "Have you eaten anything?"

"Oh, um, no." I hadn't eaten anything since dinner last night.

His lips pulled down in a frown. Next thing I knew, he was gliding the Mustang between two sedans on the side of a busy street. I have no idea how he managed to park like this. I couldn't parallel park to save my life. If it had been me, I'd have had to park three blocks over and walk to the coffee shop we were sitting in front of.

"Stay here," he said, getting out.

Even if I wanted to argue, I wouldn't have had the chance. He was striding through the glass doors of the café before I even thought of a rebuke. I didn't want to go in there anyway; there was a crowd of people. I just wanted quiet. I wanted to feel safe, like I wasn't being threatened or watched.

The cool interior of this Mustang was the closest I'd felt to safe since last night. No one would expect me to be in this car. No one would expect me not to be at work. My car was still there at the White House, so as far as everyone knew I was, too.

I leaned my head back against the buttery leather and closed my eyes. Spencer was in the line of the shop, I could see the top of his dirty-blond head. He was talking to someone easily, and the person was smiling.

He was too entirely likable.

I couldn't imagine anyone not liking Spencer. He probably had a million girlfriends.

I turned off those thoughts and shut my eyes and thought about Jack. I imagined him laughing at the monkeys' antics right now.

The next thing I knew, a car door was slamming and I jerked up, my body tensing. "It's me," he said gently, slipping two large paper cups into the center console.

I sagged back against the seat, rolling my head toward him. "I must have fallen asleep."

He dropped the brown paper sack in his lap and looked at me, pushing his sunglasses up atop his head. Golden eyes raked over me and he leaned in, running a thumb beneath my eyes where I knew there were dark circles. "Rough night, huh?"

"You have no idea," I said, relishing the brief contact. I realized then that I couldn't remember the last time someone touched me. Someone other than Jack, that is.

"Don't wanna go home, huh?"

I shook my head and bit my lower lip.

Spencer handed me a coffee and then pulled out into traffic. I took a sip of the hot liquid, realizing how thirsty I was. The coffee was sweet and creamy, and oh so good.

"Thanks for this," I said between sips. I was partially afraid to drink it as fast as I wanted for fear my stomach would revolt.

Spencer didn't say anything, but I did note the way his hand flexed over the gearshift as he moved through the streets.

Several minutes later, we pulled up to the National Mall. Usually, parking here was a nightmare, but Spencer seemed to not be plagued with that as he located and slid into a spot in mere minutes. The National Mall was two miles of open grassy space that was filled with history. Not only did it boast open spaces for biking, running, or walking your dog, but it had grand architecture.

Monuments such as the Lincoln Memorial, U.S. Capitol, and various other memorial parks. It was a popular place for tourists but also for locals.

Before climbing out of the car, Spencer handed me the paper sack. "I got you a muffin. You should eat something."

"Okay," I said, taking the bag but having no interest in actually eating.

"Come on," he said, grabbing up his coffee and getting out of the car.

Part of me was really nervous about being out here in the open. Anyone looking for me could easily find me. But then I reminded myself that everyone thought I was supposed to be at work. It didn't help me relax completely, but I no longer felt like hiding behind every trashcan we passed.

"Okay, spill," he said.

I blew out a breath. "I don't even know where to start."

He stopped and swung around abruptly to face me. "Is your boyfriend knocking you around?"

I stopped. He thought I had a boyfriend? "I don't have a boyfriend."

"Thank fuck," he muttered, dropping the glasses back down over his eyes.

"You thought I was seeing someone?" I asked, wrinkling my nose. For someone who thought I was single, he sure did do a lot of flirting. Of course, to some guys, flirting was just their natural way.

"Actually, I didn't. Everyone said you were single." His words faltered, and my eyes shot up to his.

"You asked around about me?" I don't know why, but this made me extremely giddy.

"Maybe." He shrugged. "It's my job to know about the people who work in the White House."

"Oh," I said, a little let down. Okay, I was a lot let down. He only wanted to know about my personal life because of his job.

"But what else could it be?" He went on. "You come to work with bruises and injuries, shaking like a leaf and jumping at every sound you hear. Your car doesn't have a scratch, so you weren't in an accident, and you refused to let me take you home, making me think there was some asshole there waiting who would be pissed off if he saw us together."

Okay, I saw his reasoning. It did make sense. "I'm single," I murmured, sipping the coffee, getting ready to lay it all out there.

Spencer's body tensed and he stepped close. So close I could feel the rise and fall of his chest when he breathed. "Elle. Did someone attack you?" He said the words low like the mere thought of them sickened him.

"Yes," I choked out.

He groaned and his hand tightened into a fist at his side. "Fucking fucker," he said.

Clearly, he liked the F-word.

"Did you go to the hospital?" he asked.

"No! I can't go to the hospital."

"They'll need to… uh, examine you. Make sure…"

Oh God. He thought I got raped.

"Spencer." I stopped him, placing a hand on his chest. "I wasn't raped."

His hand covered mine and wrapped around it, squeezing my fingers. "Thank fucking God," he said. "I thought I was going to go to jail for murder."

"Murder!" I said, trying to draw my hand back, but he wouldn't allow it. He kept hold of it with ease.

"I'd hunt him down and kill him." He said the words with a deadly calm tone. It was the kind of tone that made me shiver.

"I wasn't raped," I said. "But I was attacked. Last night." The tremor of fear in my voice was something I couldn't hide.

Slipping his fingers through mine, he kept hold of my hand and led me over to an isolated grassy area beneath a tree. He sat, putting his back to the tree, and through his lenses I could see his eyes sweep the area surrounding us. It made me feel safe.

I settled close to him, setting my coffee and the bag with the muffin beside us.

"Talk," he said.

I told him everything. How I couldn't sleep so I went downstairs to make some tea. I told him about the noises I heard and how they came in through my bedroom window. I shuddered to think what would have happened if they caught me sleeping.

I told him how I was dragged down the stairs, and he winced when I told him I stabbed one of them with a pen.

"What?" I said defensively. "It was better than doing nothing at all!"

"You pissed him off and he hit you in the face," he growled.

I gave him a dirty look. I wasn't letting him take away the satisfaction I got out of the one injury I was able to inflict on the guy.

I saw him open his mouth, likely to tell me what else I did that was stupid, so I spoke first to shut him up. "There's more."

The look on his face grew darker and darker as I whispered about the president, the poison, and the threats to make me do it.

"You didn't call the cops?" he asked, tossing his sunglasses on the ground beside us and running a hand over his face and head.

"They told me I couldn't. They said they had connections there."

"They were lying," he spat.

"They threatened my son," I said quietly.

A change came over him. He sat up a little bit straighter, and the rage he was emitting seemed to flat line. "You have a son?"

It didn't surprise me that Spencer knew nothing about Jack. I didn't get personal at work. I left that stuff for at home. My colleagues at the White House were just that. I went to work to do a job, not talk about why my son didn't have a father.

"You said you weren't seeing anyone," he said. "Are you married?"

"No. I'm single."

He just gazed at me.

I sighed. "Jack's father left me when I was pregnant. He barely wanted a girlfriend, let alone a surprise baby."

"How old are you?" he asked, his eyes narrowing.

"Twenty-four. Jack just turned two. He's just a baby." I got emotional just thinking about the threats being made against him.

"He just left you?" His words were hollow. I understood. It was a lot to take in. Most guys didn't see women the same way once they knew they had kids or, as many like to say, "baggage." Right about now, Spencer was probably regretting all those times he'd come into the kitchen to sneak cookies and make small talk with me.

I told myself it was better this way, that at least now he knew. At least now he wouldn't come downstairs to flirt with me, leaving me to think about him when the hour was late and I was feeling lonely.

I told myself the pain I was feeling was the bruises on my body and the cut on my head.

Basically, I did the worst thing a person could do.

I lied to myself.

"I was with him for about a year. It was pretty casual, but as far as I knew, we weren't seeing other people. The pregnancy was an accident. We'd been careful, but sometimes things happen. I didn't realize I was even pregnant 'til three months in. I told the father and he pretty much accused me of trying to trap him." I glanced away, gazing off across the grass. "His family was well off. He thought I was trying to get money or something." I shook my head, the memory of that conversation replaying in my mind.

I glanced up at Spencer and looked him right in the eye. "He walked out on me that day, and I never talked to him again. I never so much as asked for anything. I don't want anything. Jack doesn't even carry his name."

"You've been raising him alone?" Spencer asked. The look on his face was indiscernible.

"My mom helps me. She watches him during the day while I'm at work. I pay her what I can, though she never wants to take it."

"What about your dad?"

"He died before I had Jack."

He just stared at me for long moments. It made me sort of uncomfortable because I had no idea what he was thinking. Usually, when people got quiet like that, it was because they were silently judging someone else. I didn't like when people judged me. Being a single mother wasn't some curse. Even though this was the "modern" day and age, there were still a ton of judgy people out there who had no respect for a woman raising a child on her own.

"All this time you've been working all these hours at the White House and then you go home and—" He began, but I cut him off.

"Be a mom."

"I don't understand," he said, his voice growing hard.

I sighed. Clearly, confiding in Spence was the wrong thing to do. I got up to leave. I'd just call a cab. "I'm sorry I dragged you into this." I began. "I shouldn't—"

His hand caught my wrist and he pulled me around, his honey eyes searching my face. "You didn't let me finish,"

I sighed. "Look, I've had enough of judgy people. I've had, like, the worst day, and—"

He squeezed my wrist. "I don't understand how any man could leave his child," he said, completely cutting off my tirade. "How any man could walk away from you."

"What?" I said, totally sure I hadn't heard him right.

Still holding my wrist, Spencer took a few steps back until his back hit the tree, he towed me along with him, but when he stopped, I didn't. He gave me a gentle tug and I tumbled forward. His heavily muscled arms wrapped around my waist as his head dipped down.

I didn't even have to tilt up my head. His lips found mine and lifted, bringing my face up to give him total access.

A single touch.

That's all it took for me to totally melt against him. His body accepted mine and molded around me, almost like he couldn't get close enough. His lips were warm and his tongue tasted like coffee. His kiss wasn't soft and tender; he kissed me like he meant it, like kissing me was the most serious thing he'd ever done.

I'd wondered what it would be like to kiss him. I'd looked at his lips and his ornery grins for months and a sort of wistful feeling would take over the inside of my chest. But I never really thought this would happen.

I never really thought his kiss would blow the one I imagined out of the water.

How did he do it? How did he claim me with a single kiss?

He pulled my upper lip into his mouth and gently sucked at it, then released it and smoothed his skilled tongue over the swollen flesh. When he finally broke away, he didn't pull back; he merely separated our lips but rested his forehead against mine. His breathing was heavy and his chest pushed against me as we both sucked in great gulps of air.

Then he did something that totally melted what was left of me.

He grazed my forehead with a kiss and brushed his lips up along my hairline where my head was cut and kissed there, too.

My hands fisted in the fabric at his waist. My heart felt like it was going to burst right out of my chest. I was sure he could hear it hammering because it was the only sound that reached my ears.

If that wasn't enough wreckage for one kiss, he wasn't done.

Carefully, his hands slid up, his palms were so wide they completely engulfed my face as he cupped it and stared into my eyes. He didn't say a word, just looked at me. The melted honey of his eyes was thick and sweet, and then the corner of his mouth tilted up, giving me the smallest of smiles.

Slowly, still watching me, he lowered himself and planted another soft, quick kiss to my mouth.

Only then did Spencer pull completely away.

If I had any brains in my head that still worked, I might have asked him why he did that. But really, I could fucking care less.

I prayed he would do it again. I prayed he would do it longer, and when he did, we would be in private so the kiss could go a little further. I hadn't had sex in almost three years, and to be truthful, I never once missed it.

Until now.

"I had to do that," he said, his voice gravelly and low. "I couldn't concentrate on anything else."

"O—okay," I answered, a slight tremble in my voice.

He smirked, one of his dimples making a heart-stopping appearance. "And just so you know," he drawled, tucking a strand of wayward blond hair behind my ear. "I reserve the right to do it again anytime I want."

I didn't say anything. Good Lord, if I opened my mouth, I might giggle like a schoolgirl. That would be embarrassing.

"As much as I would love to keep saying things to make your face flush pink, darlin', we got a serious conversation to finish."

"Where are you from?" I asked, tilting my head and avoiding the horrible must-have conversation for just a few minutes longer.

"North Carolina."

That explained the southern twang that sometimes gave me shivers.

"So the men threatened your son?"

I nodded. "Jack. They threatened my mother, too. And my job. Basically my entire life."

He reached out and brushed the hair from my head and looked at the cut. "They hit you."

"Yeah, but this was because he shoved me and I hit my head."

Spencer's jaw clenched.

"I'm fine," I told him, resting a hand on his shoulder. "I'm more worried about my family, my son." I told him about this morning, about how they came back and took Jack, how I hadn't even heard.

I talked until my throat was sore. I told him everything. I told him about the poison I hid in the cabinet, how I lied to my mother and sent her to the zoo, and about how they trashed my bathroom. When he knew every last detail, I fell quiet, stressed and strung-out all over again.

He didn't say anything at all while I talked. Mostly, he watched me, his amber eyes intent on my face. But sometimes he would look away, scope out the area beyond us. Spencer was a watchful man, careful. He seemed to see everything with the appearance of looking at nothing. I felt safe with him. His calm, cool demeanor was assuring and smoothed the worst of my frazzled nerves.

After I fell silent, he pressed my coffee back into my hands and told me to drink it. "You need the sugar, darlin'. The lack of color in your face isn't good."

I ducked my head, self-conscious about my less-than-desirable appearance.

"Oh no you don't," he said, tipping my chin back up. "I like looking at your eyes."

"They're probably bloodshot," I rasped. My throat and voice was like a scratched record, not at all playing the way it should. So I tipped back the coffee and let some of the warmth soothe the roughness.

"Even bloodshot, those baby blues are beautiful."

"Pretty words," I murmured.

"They'd just be words if I didn't mean them," he countered.

I didn't have it in me to argue. I was beyond exhausted and scared. "I don't know what to do," I whispered, clutching the coffee.

"Yeah, darlin', I know." The compassion in his tone was almost my undoing.

"Come on," he said, scooping to pick up our stuff, then draped one of his arms across my shoulders. We walked back toward his car. If my cheek sometimes brushed against the side of his chest as we walked, I told myself it was because I was tired.

It wasn't because the idea of resting against him for even just seconds and letting someone else be strong for a moment was damned appealing.

After we were both in the Mustang with the engine running, he turned to me. "You know I can't keep this a secret." His voice was heavy with duty. "I have to elevate this. Immediately."

"I know." It was the right thing to do. The only thing to do.

But I wasn't sure it was the right thing for Jack.

My hands twisted in my lap as my stomach rolled like I was on some tiny boat in a wave-laden sea.

"Elle." Spencer's voice broke through my internal struggle. His hand covered both of mine, and I looked down at where our skin touched. "I'm not going to let anything happen to you or your son."

"I want to believe you," I whispered.

"Look at me," he implored.

Our eyes connected.

"Keeping people alive is my job. It's what I do." His eyes were intense, serious, and true.

"I hope you're good at your job," I said. I tried to make it sound like a joke but failed horribly.

"I'm the best at my job."

"Well, thank goodness for that," I said lightly as I turned to look out the window.

"Elle?" he said, still not turning away.

"Yes?"

"You're not just a job to me," he intoned. "Don't ever think you are."

I swallowed thickly, the bottom falling out of my stomach. "I'm kinda glad," I whispered, letting him in on my secret.

His teeth flashed a fast grin. "I know."

My lips pulled up into a smile. I couldn't even call him on his arrogance because he was right.

6

As soon as I told Spencer, he brought me back to the White House. I was ushered into a small office to wait while he went and told them everything he knew.

Then the interrogation started. I answered question after question. After that, I answered them again. And again. I was scrutinized by the most intimidating security team ever. Sometimes when they looked at me, I felt dirty. I felt like they thought I was some kind of twisted murder-plotting serial killer.

I wasn't.

I was a mom scared for her son. I was a woman scared for her future and a daughter scared for her mom.

I was also a woman being reeled in by a man.

Endless hours upon hours of going over every last detail until I began to doubt even myself, and through it all, Spencer was there. He didn't sit close to me or hold my hand. He didn't show any kind of feeling toward me except professional courtesy and the benefit of the doubt.

But he was still there. And sometimes in the worst moments, in the minutes I wanted to cry my eyes out, all I had to do was look at him. Those honey eyes of his pulled me back from falling off the ledge every single time.

They wanted to search my house but couldn't. They argued about that forever. Spencer was adamantly against it. They were pretty certain I was still being watched and that meant my place was, too.

I was told to keep everything in my life exactly as it always was. I wasn't to act paranoid or watchful. I was supposed to adhere to my everyday routine and do nothing that would make whoever it was that threatened me suspicious that I did what they told me not to do: tattle.

Robert Walsh, the head of the Secret Service team, was currently sitting across from me. I didn't like him. He pretended we were friends, that we had some common ground because we both worked for the president. He must have thought I was stupid. Sometimes having blond hair and being a young woman totally worked against me.

Robert thought by creating some sort of camaraderie between us, I might show him something I wasn't showing anyone else, like there was this secret part of me I kept hidden. I was so damn exhausted I couldn't hide anything if I wanted to.

"You haven't noticed anyone following you lately? Showing up to the same places you might be 'coincidentally?'" he asked.

I squeezed my eyes shut, the pain behind them drilling into my skull. "No," I answered.

He opened his mouth to ask something else, and I cut him off. "I'd like to go home now."

"Soon," he said in a completely placating tone.

"Not soon," I snapped. "Now."

"Ms. Bond," he said. I heard a hint of warning and perhaps even suspicion in his tone. But even I knew he didn't have any kind of evidence to arrest me or even hold me.

I was exhausted. I was irritable. My body hurt, and I wanted to see my son.

It was bad enough I had to call Mom and tell her I wouldn't be home early after all. I had to lie (yet again) and say there was some sort of emergency at work.

What the hell kind of food emergency could someone have? I prayed to God she didn't ask me for details.

"You said yourself that I should keep to my normal routine. If I go home too late from work, it will look suspicious. Especially so soon after they threatened me."

He sighed. He knew I was right. I basically just used his own plan against him.

"We're going to need the vial of poison they gave you," he said.

"Yes. I know." I repeated everything on autopilot. "I will bring it in first thing in the morning in the bag you gave me. I won't let anyone else touch it, and I will use the gloves you gave me to pick it up."

"I hope you know what a serious matter this is," he said gravely.

I leaned forward. "You don't think I know?" I pointed to the cut on my forehead and lifted the sleeves of my shirt to show him the bruises. "I was attacked. My son was taken from his bed and left in my car. *My car.* They want me to commit murder. I understand."

He cleared his throat. "Yes. Well…"

The door to the office opened and Spencer strode in. His suit jacket was still missing, his hair was mussed, and the gun he carried was on full display on his hip.

Even in my exhausted, emotional state, his presence sent a little zing of excitement through me.

"Her shift is supposed to be ending," he said, his eyes sweeping over me before turning away.

"You can go," Mr. Walsh said.

I sagged with relief. I didn't waste time or give him a chance to change his mind, just jumped up to leave.

Spencer grinned at my haste as I rushed toward the door.

"Ms. Bond," Mr. Walsh said.

I wanted to bang my head against the doorframe. What would it take to get away from him?

"Yes?" I turned back.

"I want to remind you that we're having your house watched. You won't see us, but we'll be there. If you try to run, if you try to—"

I made a sound in the back of my throat and held up my hand. "Stop," I snapped. "Look, I get you're just doing your job. I'm grateful and I am thankful you have assigned my house a watch and someone to also watch my son. But stop treating me like a criminal. I—" My monologue was cut short when Spencer's hand dropped onto my shoulder.

"Time to go." He ushered me out into the hall, shutting the door between Mr. Walsh and me.

I glanced up at him. "That guy is a—" Just before I slung an insult, I noted we weren't in the hallway alone, and I snapped my lips closed.

A few members of the White House staff were walking by, clearly intrigued about what was going on down here. Spencer greeted them like they'd known each other all their lives, and I took advantage and slipped away.

The sun was starting to lower in the sky as I walked through the parking lot toward my car. All I wanted to do was see Jack and get away from this place.

"Elle!" Spencer called, jogging toward me across the pavement.

When he stopped in front of me, he extended a clipboard and a pen at me. "You forgot to sign this grocery order," he said loudly.

I took the clipboard and stared down at the blank paper. Clearly, he was creating a reason to talk to me out here in the open.

"Oh!" I said in mock surprise. "I forgot." I took the pen from his hand and glanced over the blank paper like I was checking the order one last time.

"I'll stay at your place tonight," he said, low.

I glanced up swiftly, noting he was smiling widely, like he was joking with me.

But he wasn't joking. His eyes were entirely serious.

I played along, grinned, and gave a little laugh. "You can't." I hope he heard how serious I was beneath my pretend nonchalance as well.

"You shouldn't be alone." He insisted.

I glanced at the paper again and scrawled my name across the bottom. "I never have men stay over. It would look suspicious. Besides, the police are watching the house. I'll be fine."

I was rather impressed I sounded so confident. In reality, I was dreading spending all night alone in the dark.

"Elle." He began, low.

I shoved the clipboard at him and smiled widely, giving him a little wave. "I'll see you tomorrow!"

He couldn't say anything to argue; it would look suspicious. Spencer was forced to walk away, back toward the house, as I started up my car and drove away.

7

It took forever to get Jack down to sleep.

Even though I could tell he was exhausted, he fought slumber with quite the valiant effort. I spent over an hour rocking him in the chair in his room and pacing the dimly lit hallway upstairs while holding him against my chest.

It was almost as if he could read my emotions. As if he could sense all the turmoil brewing inside me. I didn't mind rocking him or singing a million little songs. I loved the time with him. I knew someday in the near future, he would be too big for me to do this with. Hell, some parents might say he was too old now, but I didn't care.

Even though rocking him was the highlight of my day and I could finally rest a little easier because I knew he was safe in my arms, I still breathed a sigh of relief when at last I was able to lay him in his crib and shake out my exhausted arms.

On nights like this, nights when I was worn out and overwhelmed, I sometimes felt sorry for myself. Sorry I was all alone, that Jack's father—that any man—had never thought I was worth sticking around for. It might be nice to have someone I could share a glass of wine with, talk about trivial stuff that happened to me that day, or even just someone I could fall asleep against while we watched unrealistic TV shows on the couch.

After watching Jack for long moments, I double-checked the baby monitor, making sure the volume was all the way up, and then went through the rest of the upstairs, checking every window for the millionth time.

It didn't matter how many times I saw they were locked; I would still be frightened.

I wanted to take a long, hot shower to release some of my insanely sore and tense muscles, but I couldn't allow myself the luxury. If I was in the shower, I wouldn't hear what was going on in the rest of the house. It would make me too vulnerable.

Instead, I settled for putting my hair in a high ponytail and washing my face quickly. I changed into an oversized T-shirt, flinging my bra across the bed, and didn't bother with any pants.

I guess there was something good about living alone.

No one knew when I went pants-less.

Once I checked on Jack yet again, I stood in the hall and debated for like ten minutes before convincing myself it was okay to go into the kitchen to get some tea and maybe a snack to bring back upstairs.

Sleep probably wouldn't happen for me tonight, but I could at least try to make myself comfortable.

The entire time I was making a mug of hot tea and milling around the kitchen, I kept sneaking glances at the high cupboard where I hid the poison. Just knowing it was there unsettled me. As much as I didn't want to get it out and put it in my purse tomorrow, I would be glad to have it out of here.

When my tea was seeping on the counter, I grabbed a granola bar out of the pantry even though I didn't want it and palmed the bottle of honey. I couldn't help but think of Spencer as I swirled the thick, sweet stuff into my tea. What was he doing right then? Probably sleeping. Lucky bastard.

After stirring the hot liquid, I licked the spoon and carried it to the sink.

That's when I saw it.

The plant.

I'd completely forgotten I dropped some of the poison into it. When it didn't die or wilt instantly, I put it out of my head.

Yesterday it was green and supple, the ivy trailing over the windowsill.

Not anymore.

It was dried, brittle, and brown. The ivy appeared like I let it sit out under the hot sun for weeks without watering it once. I reached out a finger to touch the leaves, kind of in shock they could go from perfectly healthy to dead in such a short amount of time.

Just as my finger was about to make contact with the ivy, a sound erupted in the room. I let out a startled yelp and the spoon clattered into the sink.

I spun, forgetting about the plant, to see who or what was there.

But it wasn't anyone. It was my ringing cell phone from beside my mug. With one last glance at the dead plant, I went over to stare at the screen of the phone.

I didn't recognize the number.

What the hell good was caller ID if I didn't know the number?

My heart pounded heavily as I shifted from foot to foot and debated whether or not to answer. No one ever called me at this late of an hour. Hell, no one ever called me except my mother, and I knew she was long in bed.

What if it was *them*? What if they were calling me to ask me why the president wasn't dead?

As I freaked out, the phone stopped ringing. The room was thrust back into silence.

It was probably just a wrong number.

I left all the lights on and exited the room, taking my tea, snack, and phone with me. My foot hit the bottom step and the phone started ringing again. It startled me and I jumped, spilling the hot tea down the front of my shirt.

I yelped and quickly unloaded what I was holding onto the step and pulled the saturated shirt away from my skin. Beneath it, my stomach stung from the burn.

The phone was still ringing and it pissed me off. Not only was I scared, but now I was burned, and if this ringing woke up Jack, I was going to scream.

"What?" I hissed into the line after I silenced the evil ringing.

"Elle?" answered a familiar voice.

"Spencer?" I said, surprised. All the anger drained away.

"Yeah, it's me," he said. "Did I wake you?"

"No. How did you get my number?" I asked suspiciously, still holding the shirt away.

"From your file at work," he said, like it was obvious.

"I didn't realize employee files were community property."

"They aren't."

Damned if I didn't smile at the sheepish tone of his voice.

"Why are you calling, Spence?" I asked.

"I'm outside."

"What!" I gasped, looking toward the nearest window. Of course I had all the blinds and curtains drawn so I couldn't see anything. Even if I could, he wouldn't just be standing there out in the open.

I hope.

"You aren't supposed to be here!" I hissed.

"Can I come in?" he asked, and I noticed he was trying to keep his voice low.

I couldn't exactly say no. Having a guy lurking around my property would look suspicious. And yes, okay, maybe a tiny part of me wanted him to come inside.

"What door are you at?" I asked.

"I'm not at any door yet." He paused briefly. "Turn off all the lights on the main floor like you're going upstairs for the night. Leave the back door unlocked. I'll come in after a few minutes and lock the door behind me."

"Ummm," I said, not sure I was totally comfortable with this plan. "I have all the lights on for a reason," I told him.

"I won't be seen in the dark," he said. "It's easier to hide in the shadows."

I shivered. If he was in the shadows, who else was, too?

"Elle," he whispered. The sound of my name drew all my attention to the voice in my ear. "If you don't want me to come in, say the word. I'll leave right now."

A little bit of panic rose up inside me. I didn't want him to leave. I didn't want to go upstairs and know just moments ago he'd been here, but he no longer was.

Without saying anything, I walked through the main floor and shut off all the lights. If he was as close as he said, he would know what that meant. Then I unlocked the back door.

Please, don't let this be a mistake.

I stood in the center of the kitchen, my bare feet against the cold tile, and gripped the phone to my ear, not saying a word.

He didn't say anything either.

A few seconds later, the back door creaked open. It wasn't that loud of a sound, but to me it was deafening.

Spencer quickly shut the door behind him and turned, withdrawing something from his pocket. The dim glow of his phone illuminated just a portion of his face as he held it up to shut off the call and stuffed the phone back into his pocket.

I, too, hung up my phone.

We stood there listening to the night, making sure there were no other strange sounds. When everything appeared to be fine, Spence moved quietly across the room and took my hand. His fingers were warm and they linked through my chilled ones with confidence. He tugged me through the house, moving with grace even though it was pitch black and he didn't know where any of the furniture was.

When we reached the stairs, I hurried in front of him to pick up the stuff I left on the step. When I couldn't fit it all into one hand, he reached out and took the mug, preferring to carry it for me, releasing my hand.

I forgot how intimate holding hands was.

People don't realize how singular they are. How contained their bodies are and how we mostly have a bubble of personal space around us. Holding hands with Spencer was like he defied all of that. He bypassed it by reaching into my bubble and linking us together. His fingers weaved through mine seamlessly, like it was exactly where they belonged. My personal space was invaded; that little bubble around me popped.

I didn't mind at all.

At the top of the stairs, Spence paused, not sure which way to go. I tugged him into the room on the right—my bedroom. After I dumped everything in my hand onto the bed, I left the room to once again check on Jack.

He was sleeping like a little angel, and it made me feel even more at peace.

When I left his room, I skidded to a halt in the center of the hallway. Spencer was leaning in the doorframe leading to my room. From the lamp lit in my room, I could see him for the first time since he came inside. He was dressed in a pair of low-slung dark jeans, sneakers, and a long-sleeved black waffle-knit tee.

There was a black baseball hat pulled down over his face, covering his dark-blond hair and concealing a lot of his face.

As I stared at him, he tipped his head back to stare at me from beneath the brim. "Hey," he rumbled.

"Hey," I echoed. The wet fabric of my shirt brushed my skin and I remembered I was wet, had on no pants and no bra.

I hurried toward my room, mortified and wanting to actually put on some clothes, but Spencer didn't seem to realize my haste.

I stopped short of colliding with his broad chest.

"I need to, uh, change," I said, my voice totally unsteady. He affected me in ways I'd never known. It was amazing how just his close proximity could make my body flush with heat yet also make me tremble with nerves.

"I like ya just the way ya are," he drawled.

I glanced up to where his eyes were shaded by his hat and fought the giddy sensation rising up in my middle. "I spilled tea all over my shirt. It burned me," I blurted out.

Like you couldn't have thought of anything even remotely sexy to say? I scolded myself.

This is not the time to be sexy! another voice within me shouted.

My Jekyll-and-Hyde bickering was cut short when Spencer straightened from lounging inside the doorframe and narrowed his eyes on me. "You burned yourself?"

He snatched my hand and pulled me easily into the bedroom.

"Let me see." He motioned for me to take off my shirt.

I sputtered and then laughed. "You can't actually think I'm just going to strip off my shirt."

"Why the hell not?" he demanded.

"Because it's the only thing I'm wearing?" I replied like it should have been obvious.

"Now is not the time to try and seduce me, Elle," he deadpanned. "I need to see how badly you're burned."

"I'm not trying to seduce you!" I said, incredulous.

"Good," he countered. "Then it won't matter if I take a look."

Before I could tell him what a freaking idiot he was, his hand snaked out and grabbed the hem of the shirt and lifted.

I gasped and tried to jump back. It didn't work out to well because he had a hold of my shirt. "Hold still," he scolded. "The last thing you need is any more injuries," he muttered and continued to yank up the fabric.

Total embarrassment washed over me, and I quickly folded my arms over my breasts so he couldn't lift the fabric high enough to see them.

Cool air washed over my hips and stomach as Spence reached up and slid his hat around so that he was wearing it backward and was able to get a better look at my body.

God, he looked sexy in that hat.

And from this close, I could see the scruff growing in on his jaw area. It was dark blond too and made him look totally delicious.

Holding up my shirt with one hand, he reached out with the other, gliding his fingers across my stomach, just below my ribcage. "Here?" he whispered, staring at the area.

I nodded, not bothering to glance down. The skin stung lightly as he caressed it. I didn't care. Frankly, it could hurt like hell and I still would have let him touch it. Desire suffused my limbs, making them heavy. I felt goose bumps break out over my bare skin, and maybe I should have been embarrassed at my reaction because really there wasn't anything sexual to what he was doing, but my body sure as hell acted like there was.

He frowned a little when my muscled trembled beneath him, and he glanced up. "Does it hurt?"

I shook my head, unable to speak.

"It's just red. No blisters," he answered, not looking back down at the "burn," but not pulling his fingers away either. Spencer watched me as he dragged the tops of his knuckles down the curve of my waist and moved across my navel.

"You burned anywhere else?" he rumbled in a low, throaty tone.

Man, I wish I was. I wished I could point out a thousand injuries just to give him a reason to not lift his hand.

"No," I whispered.

He glided his hand over my hip and curved his palm around the dip in my waist, tugging me just a little bit closer. Just one step… that's all I needed to take to bring my bare waist up against his body.

I tilted my head back when he bent, lowering his face toward mine. I anticipated his kiss, craved it… Part of me thought I might need it.

He stopped just inches away, his heavy-lidded eyes spearing mine. "Nice drawers," he whispered.

It took me a second to realize what he said. I was too far under his spell.

But when his lips turned up in an ornery smirk, his words penetrated my lust-laden brain. I gasped and leaped back, pulling my shirt from his hand and yanking it down over my "drawers."

"Oh my God!" I burst out. "You are such a pig!"

He laughed. "What? I was paying you a compliment."

I groaned, still yanking at the hem of my shirt. "You're making fun of me!" I challenged.

He laid a hand over his heart and looked at me solemnly. "I do swear no one wears polka dots like you do."

I. Was. Going. To. Die.

Spencer was saved from murder when Jack's cry carried across the hall. The bottom fell out of my stomach, and I raced across the hall and into his darkened room. My baby was sitting up in his crib, rubbing his eyes and fussing.

"Hey there, little man," I said gently. "What's the matter?"

He lifted his arms to me and I picked him up. Immediately, he snuggled against my chest, laying his head on my shoulder. I rocked on my feet, holding him close and letting my heart rate return to normal. His outcry scared me more than it should have, but in just a day, I'd become the most paranoid person I'd ever known.

I swayed back and forth, rubbing his back as he slipped back into sleep. I didn't put him down right away. I learned that the hard way. I had to wait until he was fully asleep before laying him back down; otherwise, he would just wake right back up again.

As I swayed, I spun around, humming softly. My movements were momentarily paused when I saw Spencer in the doorway, watching me.

Rather than say anything, I turned back around and continued rocking until I was certain he was asleep.

After Jack was back in his crib, I left the room. Spencer was no longer in the doorway. He was sitting on the end of my bed when I stepped back into my room. All the excitement and desire I felt at his touch just moments ago was dissolved into weariness.

"You look exhausted," he said quietly.

"I'm okay," I replied as I rummaged around in my dresser for some pajamas that were appropriate to wear (aka: ones with pants). Another thought of a warm shower taunted me.

I glanced at Spencer. "Do you need to leave yet?"

"You inviting me to spend the night?" he asked, wagging his eyebrows.

I rolled my eyes. "No."

"Too bad." He sighed.

"Never mind," I said, giggling at his antics.

He appeared behind me, soundless, once again crowding my personal space. "What do you need, Elle?" he asked softly.

You. I need you.

Whoa. Where did that come from?

I shook my head to clear away the thought. "I'd really like to take a shower, but I don't want to leave Jack by himself."

"I'll stay," he said. I barely heard him as air expanded his chest and it brushed against me. "Jack will be fine."

"I'll hurry," I said, taking my clothes and rushing away.

He caught my elbow and pulled me around. "Take your time. I'm not going anywhere."

In the bathroom, I sagged against the closed door.

I knew Spencer only meant he would stay until I was done in the bathroom, but I couldn't help but wish he'd meant it a different way.

8

Warm water poured over my skin, soothing some of the worst of my aches. I stood under the pressure for the first few minutes, just standing there, blinking the water from my eyes and watching it swirl around my toes. It was nice to have a few quiet minutes to myself, a few moments when I didn't have to pretend everything was okay or lie about what was really going on. Just knowing Spencer was out there making sure everything was safe for a little while was such a relief.

No, I didn't need him to do it, but sometimes I got tired of being the strong one all the time.

Still, I wasn't his responsibility and neither was Jack. So I grabbed up my coconut body wash and used my little white pouf to scrub myself down. When that was done, I took the time to shampoo and condition my hair, knowing I might not have this chance tomorrow night.

I had to force myself to turn off the water, to end the little steamy world I'd just created. Beyond this shower curtain, outside this bathroom, the real world was waiting, and quite frankly, the real world sucked ass.

Before dressing, I hurried to slather on some body lotion and gingerly apply some Neosporin to the cut on my forehead. It was turning an ugly yellow shade around the edges, so I figured it was beginning to heal. I wasn't about to take the time to blow out my long blond hair, so I smoothed some product in it and braided it in two braids that hung over my shoulders.

Once that was done, I pulled on a pair of black cotton sleep shorts and black tank top with a built-in bra. Over the tank, I added a fitted gray T-shirt, took a deep breath, and left the bathroom.

I checked in on Jack (he was fine) and then went into my room. Spencer was sitting on the edge of the bed with his cell phone in his hand.

"I didn't mean to keep you," I said, realizing he probably had better things to do than be here.

He tossed down the phone and stood. "You didn't." His eyes roamed down my body, lingering on my legs. I found myself hoping he liked what he saw.

Spence pushed off the bed and came closer. His muscles moved and shifted as he walked. He looked so powerful, almost like a predator. "You look exhausted."

"Yeah, well, it's hard to relax when people are threatening my son."

"We're going to catch these guys, Elle," Spencer swore.

"Thanks for staying while I took a shower. And for checking in," I said, not acknowledging what he said. I wanted to believe him; I truly did. But I felt like getting my hopes up would be allowing myself a false sense of safety when what I really needed was to be on guard.

Spencer stepped closer, angling his body so it aligned with mine. I could feel the heat radiating off his body, and I was tempted to lean into him. "I'm not leaving."

My eyes were fixed on the width of his chest, and when he spoke, I looked up. "You aren't?"

He shook his head. "You need sleep. You're never going to get it being here by yourself."

"There's someone watching the house." I reminded him.

"Does that make you feel safe?" he asked, his body still so incredibly close to mine.

"No." I admitted, feeling let down and weary. Being scared was exhausting.

"Do I make you feel safe?" Spencer's voice was low, calm, and steady.

Everything about him made me feel safe. It was dangerous. Feeling safe with a man meant letting down my guard. I already decided I needed to keep my guard up.

On all fronts.

"Elle?" My name rumbled out of his chest like a volcano erupting with hot lava. He tipped up my chin. "Do I?"

"Yes," I whispered. I couldn't lie. It was impossible. His eyes were like my kryptonite, like my own personal brand of truth serum.

Slowly, he bent, closing the space between us and capturing my mouth in a sizzling kiss. The second we made contact, my bones turned to mush. His lips moved over mine with tenderness, like he was asking permission for the kiss he was already taking. His gentle strokes endeared me to him, making emotion swell up within me like some kind of electrical surge in an outlet.

My chest felt tight as we continued to kiss. His lips were like pillows, like the perfect place to fall.

I made a little sound in the back of my throat, and he stilled, not lifting his mouth from mine, not breaking our contact even a little. I felt rather than saw his hands flex at his sides like he was demonstrating some kind of epic control.

"Is this okay?" he murmured against me. His lips caressed mine with every word he spoke.

"Yes." I arched just a little bit closer, my body giving him an even louder response.

Spencer wound his arms around me, tugged me up against him. His body was hard, and he wrapped himself around me. He was like a fur coat on a snowy day. An umbrella in a rainstorm. He blocked out everything except the brush of his lips and the feel of his incredible body against mine.

His tongue slid out and slipped over my lips, coaxing them open. I opened, inviting him in so my tongue could stroke against his. My knees started to tremble, desire pouring through my limbs like it never had before.

I forgot what it was like to be in someone's arms.

But as the memory came rushing back, I realized something.

It had never felt like this.

I'd never in my life felt such warring emotion. He assaulted me and protected me at the same time.

The fierce desire that wound its way through my body threatened to take me down, threatened to consume me. It was scary how just a kiss could make me feel so vulnerable.

Yet.

Yet at the same time, he made it feel okay. Okay that I was exposed to him, like he was a shield and anything that came at me would be deflected by him.

His mouth was totally gentle as it completely consumed me.

Heat suffused my insides and drowned out my thoughts. My body pushed against him, wanting even more, and he was only too happy to give it to me.

His hands traveled down to cup my butt and squeeze. Spence tilted his pelvis in to me and the steely rod between his legs could not be ignored. My God, he was hard. Rigid and unbending. What would it feel like to have that kind of strength between my legs?

Spencer's hands did not stay still; they slid upward, under the hem of my tank and T-shirt, and dragged over the skin of my lower back.

Abruptly, he pulled back, staring down at me with eyes that glowed with embers of need and stared at me with sort of an awed expression on his face.

Then, barely three seconds later, he kissed me again.

Reeling, I held on, letting the onslaught of emotions take over as his large palms moved up and around to cup my bare breasts. I gasped and he kissed me deeper, sweeping his tongue into the depths of my mouth and rubbing his thumbs over my erect nipples, causing a zing of pleasure to shoot down my body and into my core.

He ripped his mouth off mine again, and my head fell forward to rest against his chest. I gulped in great mouthfuls of air as he continued to play with my breasts.

My vagina ached. It was almost painful how much I wanted him.

The massaging movement of his hands grew gentler and then he was slipping around to my back and easing himself away so we no longer touched.

Thankfully, he kept his hands on my hips, holding me steady and saving me the embarrassment of sliding right onto the floor.

"You're killing me," he said, his voice totally hoarse. "I didn't come here to take you to bed. But if we don't stop, that's exactly what I will do."

"Then," I said, drawing in another breath, "why did you come here?"

"You need me," he answered simply. There was no smug arrogance in his voice or any kind of challenge.

Before I could tell him I certainly did not need him, he swept me off my feet.

Literally.

One minute, I was standing on still trembling legs, and the next, he was holding me. "You need sleep. The only way you're going to get it is if I make sure."

With one strong pull, he peeled the covers of the bed away and laid me against the cool sheets. My body melted against the mattress because it felt so wonderful to lie down.

I started to sit up. "I can't."

He pushed me back down. "You can."

I shook my head. "I'm going to sleep in Jack's room."

"No," he said firmly, pulling the covers over me. "You aren't."

"Don't you tell me what to do!" I snapped.

He grinned. "I like a feisty woman."

I glared at him. I couldn't help but stare at the way his hair was flopping in his eyes.

"I'll sleep in his room," Spencer said.

"You can't."

"Why not?" He raised an eyebrow.

"Jack doesn't know you. You'll scare him."

"I didn't realize Jack would see me."

"Jack isn't your responsibility." I argued.

"You are," he retorted.

Shock rendered me speechless. Why would he think that? Spencer lowered himself on the side of the bed beside me. "Get some sleep, Elle. You need it." He brushed the back of his hand over my cheek as he spoke.

I yawned.

He smiled.

"I'll make sure everything is safe."

Maybe I'd just lie here a few minutes. This bed really was comfortable…

Beside the bed, Spencer switched off the lamp, and I felt his lips brush over my hairline. Not once, but twice.

Maybe I was just so exhausted I couldn't fight sleep another second, or maybe it was knowing he was there that made me slip into blissful oblivion.

9

Blissful oblivion is overrated.

At least murderous criminals seemed to think so.

My body was heavy. Sleep was like a drug rendering me immobile, when a tiny noise first echoed through the room.

It wasn't enough to alert me that something could be wrong.

The soft footfalls across the carpet intruded on the heavy curtain of slumber that draped me, yet it didn't seem to be enough.

I slept on, not knowing how close danger really was.

A rough hand assaulted my shoulder, squeezing until the bone felt like it might break. I woke with a sudden start, like I spent too long without oxygen and my body gulped it in with desperation.

As my brain was trying to assimilate what was happening, he flipped me over and pinned me to the mattress. Pain lanced through me like the sharp cut of a sword, and I opened my mouth to scream, to alert Spencer.

But a heavy hand beat me to it.

He slapped his palm over my mouth and dug his fingers into the sides of my face. I felt his nails dig into my flesh, and my eyes opened in horror when he straddled me on the bed.

I tried to buck him off, to kick and yell, but he was entirely too heavy, and then he pulled out a blade.

The moonlight filtering through the now open window glinted off the steel blade and caught my attention. How something so shiny and smooth could be so deadly I didn't understand.

The man held it up for me to see, a silent threat. His heavy weight pinned me and his hand was suffocating. So much so, I began to panic. My lungs began to seize, so I pleaded with him, trying to put every ounce of desperation I felt into my eyes.

Beneath the black ski mask, his teeth flashed white with his nasty smile.

"I told you to kill him," he growled, leaning in close. It was dark in my room, but even still I could see the blue in his eyes.

I always associated the color blue with the cloudless sky and an endless ocean. From this moment on, it would always be the color of death.

I shook my head, trying to make some excuse for the reason I had to commit murder, but his beefy hand blocked my mouth.

Once again, I remembered I couldn't breathe.

In desperation, I bit down, catching the fleshy part of his finger. He gave a roar and lifted his hand. Greedily, I sucked in air as I silently thanked him for making such a loud noise.

Spencer would barrel through the doorway any minute.

Spencer would help me.

Spencer never came.

"If you won't do the job," the man growled, "then there is no reason to let you live."

He raised the blade high above his head, with the wicked-looking end pointing down at my chest.

I started to scream. The guttural sounds ripped through my vocal chords, vibrating everything in my throat.

My shriek didn't deter him.

In fact, I think it excited him.

The blade slashed down, and I closed my eyes, not wanting to witness my own bloody murder.

"Elle!" Spencer called my name urgently. My body was flopping around like a lifeless ragdoll.

My eyes shot open and my body registered two large hands digging into my shoulders, pinning me down.

I started screaming again.

"*Fuck*," he swore.

He released my body, and I fell against the bed, but I didn't stay there. He lifted me completely and began walking with me in his arms. He strode across the hallway and into the bathroom, where he reached behind the shower to turn on the water.

The sound of water pressure seemed to break through my panic.

My eyesight seemed to clear just as Spencer flung back the curtain to step under the spray.

"Wait!" I gasped, stiffening in his arms. "I don't want to go in there!"

I stopped and looked down. His entire face was grim and shadowed.

"I'm sorry," I whispered, mortified. "I must have been having a nightmare."

"That was some fucking nightmare," he muttered, turning off the water and moving out of the bathroom.

Without me asking, he carried me into Jack's room and stood beside the crib so I could stare down at my sleeping son.

At least someone was still experiencing blissful oblivion. Thank God I hadn't woken him.

When I sagged back against Spencer, he left Jack's room and carried me back into mine.

"I thought you were being fucking murdered in here," he muttered. "You started screaming, and I almost jumped out of my skin."

"It felt so real," I whispered, still seeing the blue eyes of my killer so clearly.

"I know, darlin'," he said, low, his voice taking on a buttery tone.

Instead of putting me back in bed, he sat down with me in his lap and scooted so he was leaning against the headboard and I was leaning against him.

"Want to tell me about it?" he asked, rubbing my back.

I shuddered. "No."

"Fair enough," he rumbled.

I curled into his chest, my body automatically seeking out his shelter. By the time I realized what I'd done, I was already snuggled against him with his arm holding me in place.

After long silent moments, I said, "You can go home, try and catch some sleep if you want. I doubt I will be getting any more sleep tonight."

He grunted. "Yes, you will."

"How do you know?"

He used his free arm to reach around behind us. He arched his back a little, then withdrew it. In his hand was a black pistol. His hand gripped it skillfully, his finger just shy of the trigger. "Because this gun says so," he murmured, laying it on the bed right beside his leg. "If anyone comes close to this house, to you or to Jack, I will fucking shoot them dead."

"You say the F-word a lot," I muttered, listening to the sound of his steady heartbeat.

"Yep," Spence agreed.

I felt sleep slowly reach out to me, pulling me back into its clutches. My body jerked suddenly, protesting the attempt.

Spencer wrapped his other arm around me so he totally encompassed me, and his chin rested on the top of my head. "I got you," he murmured.

It was all he needed to say…

The next thing I knew, my alarm was chirping at me. I groaned and reached for it, shutting it off and then snuggling back into the pillow.

Another day. The thought drifted through my mind gloomily before I remembered last night.

And Spencer.

I sprang up like a Jack-in-the-box, sending my covers flying, and raced out of my room and into Jack's.

His room was dim because of the blackout curtains over his window, so I couldn't see inside his crib until I was right beside it.

It was empty.

My knees almost buckled as I whimpered.

Not again.

No, no, no. Not again.

I raced down the stairs and grabbed my keys by the door. It took me a minute to unlatch all the locks, but when I did, I threw the door open so hard it banged against the wall.

Please, let him be in the car again.

"Elle." Spencer's voice stopped me cold. I spun around, ready to tell him about Jack.

But I didn't have to.

Spencer was standing in the doorway of the kitchen, holding Jack. Both of them were staring at me.

I gave a cry of relief and rushed through the room and scooped Jack out of Spencer's arms, hugging him tight.

Jack wasn't impressed. He began to wiggle and squirm, trying to get out of my tight hold.

"I guess I should have woken you," Spencer said, watching me.

"What the hell are you doing?" I demanded.

Jack gave a shout, pulling my attention toward him. "No," he said, telling me his favorite word. Then he held his arms out to Spencer and leaned toward him.

Shock rippled through me.

He wanted Spencer?

Spencer gave Jack a grin and then glanced at me. "He woke up. I was going to get you, but he didn't seem to mind me so I brought him downstairs with me while I was making coffee."

Jack was still trying to get to Spencer so I nodded. Spencer grabbed him and tucked his arm under Jack's diaper-clad butt and held him up. Jack looked up at Spence with a toothless grin.

"I think I'm in trouble with Mom," Spencer told my son.

Jack grinned.

He liked him.

Jack liked Spencer.

He was staring up at him like Spencer hung the moon or something. It made this tight knot form in my throat. I always told myself Jack not having a father, or any kind of father figure in his life, was no big deal. I told myself that having my mom and me as caretakers was more than enough and the love we gave him would overshadow the lack of a man in his life.

I always believed that.

Until now.

There was no way I could see Jack and Spencer standing there grinning at each other, rumpled sleep clothes and mussed hair, and not be affected.

I was a horrible mother. My son was going to grow up with a void in his life that could only be filled by a father.

I hated the man who got me pregnant in that moment. Well, okay, I hated him every moment of the day. But right this second, it was way more intense.

How could he walk away from such a beautiful little boy? His dark hair and hazel eyes were practically sinful. And his chubby cheeks and easy grin infected you with nothing but love and warmth.

"Elle?" Spencer said, a frown marring his face.

I cleared my throat. "Sorry," I muttered. "It just scared me."

"I'm sorry. I thought you would sleep a little longer. I was going to bring him back upstairs."

"It's okay," I said, still feeling the grip of mom guilt as I strode farther into the kitchen for a mug. I needed coffee.

I took a deep breath of the intense aroma and felt a little bit of release in my already tight muscles. After I poured myself and Spencer a mug, I turned.

Jack was sitting in his booster seat, picking up Cheerios off the table and sticking them into his mouth.

"I hope it's okay," Spencer said, sheepish. He grabbed the mug I poured him and took a sip. "He pointed at them."

"You're good with kids?" I asked, mildly surprised.

He shrugged. "My sister has a couple little rug rats. Hers all eat Cheerios, too." Spencer's voice held a note of fondness when he talked about his family, and it made my stomach do a little flip.

"It's fine," I said, still watching Jack shovel in the dry cereal.

I abandoned my coffee to get Jack a sippy full of milk. Once he was drinking it happily, I turned back to Spencer. "You like scrambled eggs?"

"I like anything you're making." He ambled over to the coffee pot and refilled his mug. I couldn't help but notice his feet were bare and his shirt was rumpled. It was sexy as hell.

"Did you sleep at all?" I asked, trying to focus on getting out everything I needed for breakfast.

"Yep. I'm good," he replied. "Can I help with anything?"

I handed him a banana and a knife. "Here, feed some of this to Jack. Cut it up small so he doesn't choke."

I waited for him to protest.

He didn't.

Instead, he settled beside Jack with his coffee, propping his bare feet up on the chair across from him, and began to feed my son.

When I failed to do anything but stand there and smile, I earned a lazy grin. "You want a bite?" Spencer said, lifting his eyebrow.

For some reason, I didn't think he meant of the banana.

I spun swiftly and worked quickly. In no time, I had eggs scrambling, bread toasting, and bacon sizzling.

Once it was all heaped onto a plate, I sat it in front of Spencer and handed him a fork. "I- I'm not used to seeing a man here. Or with Jack."

I started back to the island, but he caught my wrist. I looked at him.

"How long you been single, Elle?" he asked quietly.

"Since *he* left us."

"You haven't dated at all?" Why did he seem surprised?

"Of course not," I said, going back to make myself a much smaller plate. My stomach revolted at the idea of food, but I was going to eat it. I needed fuel to get through the day. "I don't have time to date. And as soon as most guys figure out I'm not exactly alone, they don't hang around."

"What the hell kind of men are you meeting?" Spencer muttered as he shoved an epically large bite into his mouth.

"I'm not meeting any," I retorted, watching him chew. "I don't have time for a man. My son and my career are all I have room for."

He looked up. His amber eyes focused on mine. "What if the right guy came along?"

Was he saying he was the right guy?

My heart screamed, *Yes, yes, yes!*

I reminded it that this was not some weird commercial for shampoo.

I was saved from answering when Spencer's cell went off.

"Yeah?" he said into the line.

He listened for a moment and then glanced at me. "I'm doing it now."

Another pause.

"Yeah, I know. It wasn't a good time."

I couldn't help but wonder who he was talking to.

"Yeah, I did," Spencer said, an underlying threat to his words. "It was necessary."

A few minutes and a few grunts later, he hung up.

"Is something wrong?" I asked when he started eating again.

"Nope."

Jack reached for the remaining half of the banana, and Spencer snatched it up before I could and cut it swiftly into small chunks. Jack started shoveling it into his mouth with gusto.

"I need to get the poison from you, Elle," he said quietly.

I nodded. "Yeah, I said I'd bring it in today."

He shook his head. "I'd like to take it now. I'm going to drop it off at a private lab before I go in to work. They're going to rush the results."

I felt like an idiot.

It never occurred to me that Spencer came here last night because he wanted something. I was stupid. I blindly thought he had come because he wanted to check on me. I thought he came because he cared.

I pushed away from the table and stood under the high cabinet I put it in. "It's up there." I pointed. "You can reach it better than me."

He nodded. "I'll get it."

I felt awkward suddenly. The little moment I'd been living in at the breakfast table was popped.

It was for the better.

"Oh, um," I said, drawing his attention. "I put some of the poison on my plant," I pointed to the dead, brittle thing. "As you can see, they didn't lie about what it is."

His mouth flattened into a grim line. His plate was empty when he stood and strode over to the cabinet and pulled down the vial of poison.

"Sick bastards," he muttered.

Jack, who had clearly eaten his fill, started launching cereal around the kitchen.

I pulled out the evidence bag Mr. Walsh gave me and handed it to Spencer. "You can put it in here."

"Elle," he said, taking the bag, "about last night…"

"I get it," I said. "They wanted you to bring in the sample. Walsh doesn't trust me."

"Walsh is all about the job."

"Aren't you?"

"Usually," he said cryptically.

"Well, I hope you didn't get in too much trouble for not bringing it in right away."

"It's all good," he said. "They understand."

Well, at least someone does, I thought.

Figuring that Jack made enough of a mess for one morning, I lifted him out of his seat and held him out. "You are a messy boy," I told him, laughing.

He grinned and laughed. Then he started kicking his feet around, wanting me to put him down. "Don't go far," I told him, setting him down. "You need to get dressed."

He toddled over to where Spencer was and stared up at him. Spencer gave him a lopsided grin.

My heart turned over.

"You should probably get that to the lab," I said, motioning toward the bag. It made me slightly uncomfortable that Jack seemed to like Spencer so much. It was one of the reasons I didn't date. I didn't want Jack getting attached to someone who wasn't going to stick around.

"I need to wait until after you leave before I can clear out," he replied. "Whoever is watching the house and you will likely stay with you. Once you're gone, they won't notice me leave."

I nodded. It was something I hadn't even thought about. "Okay. Well, we're going to go get dressed."

"Need some help?" he asked, wagging his eyebrows at me.

I laughed. "No."

"Can't blame a guy for trying," he called out as Jack and I left the room.

I smiled.

I definitely couldn't.

10

I wasn't allowed in the kitchen. Once inside the walls of the White House, I was ushered into another part of the house, where I was questioned all over again about everything. Most of my morning was spent replaying what I did after work the night before and if I was paid a visit again. I knew they only wanted to trip me up, or for me to recall a detail I'd forgotten, but damn, how many times could I say the same thing?

"You have someone watching my son?" I probed, interrupting whatever he wanted to ask next. If they could ask questions twenty times, then so could I.

"Yes, Ms. Bond, your son and mother are under surveillance. No harm will come to them," he answered patiently.

In truth, it didn't make me feel any better. My house still felt like a dangerous cage. I felt like my son and I were being used for bait to catch these criminals. No one ever said that, but I knew. I knew my life, Jack's life, wasn't as important as the commander in chief's. I didn't think it was fair, but it was the way it was.

The door opened and I looked up. My entire body cried out with relief when I saw Spencer. He didn't glance at me. He kept his expression sober and focused on Robert Walsh. He was dressed like always, a black suit with a white shirt.

"The results are back from the vial she brought in from her house," Spencer told him.

"Good. I'll go look at them now." Robert got up and left the room without another word.

As soon as he was gone, I slumped back into the seat, utterly defeated. Spencer quietly shut the door, closing us in the room together. Finally, he looked at me, taking in my entire body, and then crouched down in front of my chair, resting his hand on my knee.

"Long day?" he asked.

"You have no idea." I groaned. I looked at him. "They think I'm somehow in on this. They think I'm guilty."

His gaze grew dark. "No, they're just doing their jobs. No one thinks you want to kill the president."

"I'm so tired," I whispered, tears filling my eyes.

"I know, darlin'," he crooned and swept me out of the chair and sat down, fitting me into his lap.

Normally, I might have protested, but I didn't have it in me. Instead, I breathed in that deep scent of his and pressed my face against his neck. I tried to stop the tears from coming, but they leaked out anyway. I knew he could feel them. My face was right against his skin, but he didn't say anything.

All I could think about was Jack and my mom. If they were safe, if someone was watching them. The questions were relentless. The look of doubt behind Walsh's eyes. And I hated lying. I had to lie to everyone. My mom, my co-workers… no one could know about this.

Slowly, he rubbed slow circles over my back and brushed his fingertips through my wavy hair. I didn't have much energy when I got ready this morning, so I just released the braids and let my hair down in the loose beachy waves the braids left behind.

"It will be over soon," Spencer murmured. I didn't know what I would do without him here. I would surely have fallen apart by now. Just his mere presence, knowing he was on my side, made a world of difference.

"They won't even let me in the kitchen to cook. I can't even distract myself with work." I complained.

"It's a damn shame," he drawled as his stomach rumbled loudly.

A muffled giggle forced its way out of my throat, and I tipped back my head, still lying on his shoulder, to look up at him. "Are you hungry?"

"All the cookies in the kitchen are gone," he said, sheepish.

I smiled. "I'm sure someone else has been making them in my place."

"They have. They don't taste good." He made a face.

Some of the storm clouds in my heart seemed to blow away. Even when he was complaining, he was utterly charming.

"I doubt that. Everyone in that kitchen cooks very well."

"Well, they aren't your cookies and those are the only ones I like."

"Are you using flattery to make me feel better?" I teased.

He grunted. "It's not flattery if it's the truth."

"Thank you," I whispered, rolling my head back into his neck. His body was so strong-feeling. Solid. I was resting all my weight on him, not bothering to try and hold myself up. He didn't even shift. It was like my weight was nothing for him to bear. All morning it felt like I was standing on shaky ground.

But not now.

Right now I felt incredibly secure.

"For what?" he asked softly, bringing his arms around to loop around my waist.

"For being here."

"How's Jack?" he asked, his tone casual.

My body stiffened slightly because he was asking about my son. I sat up, my eyes widening and my heart beginning to pound. "Did something happen?" I started to scramble off his lap, but his arms were like iron vises and wouldn't let me move.

"Calm down, darlin'," Spencer drawled. "Everything's fine. I was just asking about your boy."

"Oh." I studied his face a moment. His eyes were sincere. "Sorry, I'm not used to people asking about him."

"Well, he's part of you and that means I'm going to ask about him."

Something in my heart caved in a little. Like the soft spot that I managed to fill in with loosely packed dirt caved in unexpectedly.

"He's good," I replied. "With my mom."

Spencer's palm found the back of my head and he guided it back down to his shoulder. "He's a cute kid."

"I just want this to be over," I whispered.

The door pulled open, the footsteps coming into the room faltered, and my body stiffened. Spencer probably wasn't supposed to be in here with me. He definitely wasn't supposed to be holding me in his lap. The last thing I wanted to do was get him into trouble.

I started to leap up, but Spencer did that vise thing again with his arms, refusing to let me go.

"What did you find?" he asked, totally casual, like he wasn't holding me. He didn't seem the least bit embarrassed he was caught.

Mr. Walsh cleared his throat and stared at us for long seconds before answering. I knew he could see the way my cheeks were flaming with embarrassment.

"It's what she says. Untraceable poison. Highly toxic. Will kill immediately. Her prints are all over the bottle."

This time Spencer did stiffen, and when I jumped up, he didn't stop me. "That's because I touched it, when I hid it in my cabinet." I defended.

Mr. Walsh sighed and held up his hand. "I realize that, Ms. Bond."

"It probably didn't have any other prints because those men were wearing gloves," I said, even though I'd told them that at least five hundred times.

"You going to try and pin this on her, Walsh?" Spencer said, his tone completely no-nonsense and cold. He rose up out of the chair, unfolding his impressive height and width.

"Don't get your panties in a bunch, Waller. We found another print as well, only a partial and so small we'll never be able to run it."

"But you said…" I echoed, feeling sick.

"I said there weren't any prints. There weren't. No viable ones anyway," he muttered and slapped down a manila folder on the desk. I jumped at the sudden burst of sound.

"I think she's had enough," Spencer said, putting a hand to the small of my back. "She's told you everything."

"A million times," I muttered.

Spencer covered a laugh with his cough.

Mr. Walsh studied me for long moments, then sighed dejectedly. "Yeah." I watched as he scrubbed a hand over his craggy features and then plopped down in the black leather chair behind the desk. "What a fucking clusterfuck."

Apparently Spencer learned his fowl language here at work.

"You can't go home 'til your normal time," he said. "We don't—"

"Want it to look suspicious." I finished. "Yeah, I know."

He had the grace to cringe.

"You can't go back onto normal kitchen duty," he said, reminding me that while he might not think I'm totally guilty, he wasn't ready to declare I *wasn't* either.

"We need cookies," Spencer said. "She can go make some."

"You can't be cooking for the first family," Walsh said, no apology in his tone.

"Good. More for me," Spencer said good-naturedly.

I was standing there trying not to be angry that I was still suspected of trying to poison people.

Walsh looked between Spencer and me. Then he sighed. "What kind you making?" Walsh directed the question at me.

"Chocolate chip," Spencer answered.

I raised my eyebrows at Mr. Walsh and said, "Apparently, chocolate chip."

"All right," he sighed. "Go." He waved his hands at the door as he spoke.

Spencer went around me to pull open the door and hold it open. I stepped out into the hall, feeling like a freed inmate

"Waller, I want to talk to you," Walsh said from inside the room.

I grimaced and looked at Spencer. He was probably going to get a lecture for consorting with a suspected criminal.

Spencer didn't seem concerned. He winked. "Go make my cookies, woman."

I couldn't help but smile as I walked away, down the hall. Seconds later, the door to the office closed and another suit-wearing agent fell into step beside me.

I gave him a glance. He looked at me with no expression.

"You were told to watch me?" I asked without heat.

He nodded once.

I wasn't surprised, not at all.

"Well, come on, then, warden," I said, heading to the kitchen and resigned myself to being watched like a hawk for the rest of the day.

11

Generally speaking, cookies make everyone happy.

Unless, of course, you are a Secret Service agent with a stick up your ass.

After spending endless hours being questioned and scrutinized, I was tired of gloomy, constipated expressions. I thought finally being allowed to escape to the kitchen would be a relief. Instead, I got stuck with a guard who probably wouldn't crack a smile to save his life.

It led me to believe two things:

1.) He really thought I was guilty and was pissed he had to babysit me.

or...

2.) He really was constipated and mad he couldn't go to the bathroom.

I was going to go with the latter because I literally could not make a move or add an ingredient to the mixing bowl without him watching like a hawk. It became crystal clear that he was sent to make sure I didn't poison anyone.

Frankly, I was offended.

I mean, who in their ever-loving mind would uncover a plot to poison the president and then go into the kitchen and make poisoned cookies?

Actually, that was probably already an episode on some weird crime drama on TV.

I felt my shoulders slump a little. I understood why I was being watched. I was surprised they were letting me anywhere in the kitchen. Of course, I was in the small kitchen off the large one. I was alone (except for ol' Hawk Eyes, of course), and I had already been told no one could eat what I made. Except for Spencer, of course. He was eating at his own risk.

The spatula I was using to incorporate the chocolate chunks into the dough clattered against the porcelain when I dropped it. Realization dawned.

I was going to get fired.

It didn't matter that I was innocent. It didn't matter that I told the truth. It didn't matter that I literally had been studying culinary arts since the age of seventeen, having graduated a year early and then dedicated my life to working my way up to this job. All the time I spent sacrificing my free time and then later my time with my infant son so I could advance my career and have a solid background to take me into my thirties... it was all for nothing.

I was ruined.

My dishes, no matter how artfully prepared, would be tainted in suspicion.

"Miss?" the watchman said as I sniffled.

"Sorry," I said, grabbing a nearby napkin and wiping my eyes. After rewashing my hands, I scooped out equal-sized cookies (I used an ice cream scoop, makes the perfect size every time) and slid them into the already heated oven.

I busied myself cleaning up the minimal mess I made and became rather irritated that whenever I shifted, so did the man assigned to me. He kept my hands in view at all times. I could have made it harder for him, but why bother?

Besides, I didn't have anything to hide, and acting like a child was plain stupid.

The little timer on the oven went off, and I pulled out two large cookie sheets from the double ovens and set them on the stone counter. After letting them cool on the sheet for a couple minutes, I began sliding them off one by one with a metal spatula and onto a cooling rack. Once that was done, I slid the cookie sheets into the industrial-sized washing machine and grabbed a large white platter to put them on when they were cool.

The air was scented with the sweet smell of chocolate and sugar. It reminded me of when I was little and my mom and I would bake in the kitchen together. She always measured out the ingredients, and then I would add them to the bowl. She never minded when I ate the cookie dough, even though they say you aren't supposed to because of the raw egg. Eating the dough was always half the fun of baking.

It was something I always planned to do with Jack. Those were the kind of memories I wanted him to have. That is if I somehow wasn't wrongfully indicted for conspiracy to commit murder.

I felt bone weary, like all I wanted to do was lie down and let my body sink into the mattress of my bed. I wanted to hold my son and see his little chubby cheeks and listen to his baby babbling.

Instead, I was standing here in the kitchen of a job I was totally getting fired from because they suspected I might be a murderer.

Oh, and I was baking cookies.

Yep. This was the life.

I glanced down at the cooling treats and back at the man watching me. "Cookie?" I asked politely and held one out.

He actually recoiled.

Yep. He didn't trust me.

I sighed heavily, and it was laced with some anger. "Really?" I said. "You just stood there and stared me down while I was making them. You really think I somehow ninja-ed some kind of deadly ingredient in them?"

His face blanched. Then he recovered to say, "I can't eat while I'm on the job."

I laughed. Spencer ate constantly. Like the man was always chewing something. I wouldn't be surprised if all his suit pockets were filled with snacks.

"Okay." I shrugged and broke the cookie in half. I took a huge bite and sighed. "I love when the chocolate is still all melty," I said dreamily.

In truth, I wasn't the least bit hungry, but I'd be damned if I'd stand here and let this douche bag insult me.

His serious face pulled down into a frown. I shoved the rest of the cookie into my mouth and licked the chocolate off my finger.

He glanced at the rack.

"Sure you don't want one?" I said.

His eyes snapped back up to mine. "No."

Spencer appeared, waltzing through the door like he owned the place. The tie around his neck was loosened and slightly askew, and he looked a little tired. But that didn't stop him from giving me a smile that said he was happy to see me.

My tummy flipped over, and I smiled. He made me feel good. Even in the midst of all this chaos, Spencer was the silver lining.

He glanced over at the man standing there and then back at me. I raised my eyebrows but said nothing. He looked at the island covered in cookies and groaned.

He didn't even think about it.

He just scooped one up and shoved the entire thing in his mouth.

Joy burst in the center of my chest and flowed outward. It brought with it a feeling of peace. Clearly, not everyone thought I was trying to kill them with cookies. It was like the thought never even crossed his mind.

Constipated man stiffened and stared at him as if he were going on alert, ready to jump into action when Spence collapsed on the floor in a heap.

Spencer noticed the man's odd behavior and turned to look at him. Then he glanced at me. I shrugged. He grabbed up another cookie and bit into it.

"What?" he asked the man.

He cleared his throat. Spencer regarded him coolly as he shoved the rest of the cookie into his face. He turned to me. There was melted chocolate smeared on the corner of his lip.

It was adorable.

It was also wholly enticing. I wanted to lick it off.

There was a question in his eyes.

"Your friend here thinks I poisoned what you're eating."

Spencer's eyes narrowed into slits. He reached out and grabbed yet another cookie and turned to stare at the man. He glared at him silently, his gaze intimidating and hard. Then he shoved the entire cookie into his mouth and chewed, still staring.

"Langdon," Spencer admonished, still chewing. "I thought you were better than that, man."

Langdon had the grace to look embarrassed.

It gave me silent pleasure.

Abruptly, Spencer turned away and looked at me, winking. "More for me," he said, then scooped up about four more.

"Can I talk to you a second?" he asked.

I nodded.

He glanced at Langdon and then took me gently by the elbow and pulled me across the kitchen. Langdon followed us with his eyes. Spencer looked at him and said, "Case stuff."

Langdon nodded and glanced at the floor.

"I wanted to tell you I'm not going to be around the rest of the day," he said, his fingers caressing the inside of my elbow.

"Okay," I replied. It was disappointing because Spencer was the only one in my corner, but I realized he had a life and needed time to live it.

He released my arm and shoved a hand through his hair like he was bothered by my reaction. "I'm not going to be able to stay at your house tonight either," he said, his voice whisper quiet.

I swallowed. "Of course not," I said reasonably. "You already got the poison."

"Fuck," he muttered.

I couldn't really understand what made him mad.

"Stop acting like that," he growled.

"Acting like what?" I blinked.

"Like you don't care."

My tongue burst out to wet my lips. "Spence—" I began.

He cut me off by shoving another cookie in his mouth and holding up a finger. After several moments of chewing, he said. "You know damn well I didn't come over last night just for that stuff."

"But…"

He held up his hand again. Clearly, this was going to be a one-man conversation.

"Yeah, I was asked to come get it. But I was also told to bring it in right away. I wasn't supposed to stay."

"Spencer!" I gasped, drawing the eye of Langdon. I lowered my voice. "Then why did you?"

He stared at me intently, his eyes like liquid honey. "I think you know."

Little shivers of excitement raced up my back.

He grabbed my hand, lacing our fingers together. "There's something between us, Elle. There has been for a long time. And it's definitely more than work."

"You mean you don't just like my cookies?" I smiled sweetly at him.

He grinned. "You could never make another cookie again, and I would still find reasons to come in this kitchen to see you."

Sadness enveloped me. "You know I'm going to get fired, right?"

"We're going to work this out," he said solemnly. "But even so, I know where you live."

I couldn't help but smile.

"So yeah." He shoved another cookie into his mouth. "I can't come by tonight because I have to work. Presidential stuff."

Stuff he was likely told not to tell me. I nodded. "I'll be okay."

"I made them put another man on your house. You're going to be fine, okay?"

I nodded, mustering my bravery. I would be fine. I could take care of myself and Jack. Then I thought of something. "Spence?"

"Hmm?" he said around a mouthful of his last cookie.

"Did you get in trouble before? Is Walsh upset about…?" My voice faded away, I wasn't really sure what to call what was going on between Spence and me.

"Our relationship?" he supplied, totally comfortable calling it that.

I could only nod. Did we have a relationship?

"It's not exactly a secret I like your cookies." He grinned suggestively.

I smiled. "Well, up until today, my *cookies* were never in your lap."

"He'll get over it," Spencer muttered.

I knew then that he likely did get a lecture, and that whatever work he had tonight was probably a direct result of the closeness between us.

I might take comfort in being around Spencer, but it wasn't good for him. I was going down and it wasn't fair to drag him down with me. I didn't want him being labeled as someone who conspired with the deadly chef.

Robert Walsh rushed into the room, stopping abruptly, his eyes going right to me. There was a certain wildness about him, a ruffling of his usually calm feathers. My anxiety went through the roof. Immediately, my heart began to hammer and my breathing came in short spurts.

Something was wrong. I could sense it.

"What happened?" I gasped, walking away from Spencer.

"There's been an incident," he said, grave.

"Mr. President?" Spencer asked, his voice sounding hollow.

Mr. Walsh shook his head and looked at me. "Not the president."

"No," I said, shaking my head. Dread was like a lead weight threatening to pull me down deep. Spencer was at my side instantly, his arm winding around my waist, supporting my already sinking body.

Walsh frowned. "It's Jack."

12

I rushed upstairs and into the little office where I left my bag this morning. I could hear my cell phone ringing from the opposite end of the hall.

I started to run.

The ringing of the phone silenced, and I gave a strangled cry because I didn't make it, but as I barreled through the doorway, it began ringing again. The contents of my bag scattered all over the floor as I upended it to get to my phone.

"Hello," I gasped into the line. I was completely out of breath from running up the stairs and down the hall.

"Elle," my mother said into my ear.

"What's the matter?" I demanded.

I was aware of Spencer and Mr. Walsh coming in the room behind me, but I didn't turn to see them. I was pissed at Robert, and if I looked at him again, I might claw out his eyes.

How could he come into the kitchen like that, tell me there was an incident concerning my son, but report he didn't have the details? He clearly didn't have kids or else he never would have done something so dire. He did yell after me that Jack was safe, but the damage was already done.

I needed to get to my son as soon as possible.

"Everyone's fine," Mom rushed to say. "But something odd happened."

"Jack's okay?" I said, needing to be sure.

"Yes, honey, he's fine," she said. "Hold on a second."

There was a very brief pause, and then I heard her voice in the background. "Tell Mommy hi."

"Jack?" I said, my voice cracking.

"Ma!" he said and then started babbling things I didn't understand.

I started crying and sank down into the nearest chair. Hearing his voice was like a dam breaking on an overfull stream. I swallowed down the worst of my reaction, realizing I wasn't alone and not wanting to make Jack upset with my blubbering.

"I miss you," I told him, trying to inject some cheerfulness in my tone. "I'll be home in just a little bit."

"Tell her bye," Mom said in the background, and my heart broke a little bit. I wasn't ready to let him go.

"Bye-bye," Jack said into the line. His innocent voice filled my head and caused new tears to well.

"Bye, baby. Love you," I said. I didn't care if the president himself was listening. I always told my son I loved him no matter what.

"See," Mom said, taking back the phone. "He's fine."

"What happened, Mom?" I said, my voice leaving no room for half answers and excuses. I felt all eyes on me, and I decided rather than repeat this conversation over a million times to switch her on speaker.

I glanced at everyone, making a silent motion with my finger against my lips, and they all nodded.

"I took him to the aquarium, like we talked about," she said. I nodded even though I knew she couldn't see me. It was more or less me telling myself I remembered. Ever since the men invaded my home the other night, I'd been suggesting (and paying for) various outings for her and Jack, thinking the crowd would help keep them safe.

It seemed I was wrong.

"We were in the gift shop, and he was going crazy for this stuffed turtle up on one of the high shelves, so I turned to grab it, and when I turned back he was gone."

My stomach twisted violently, and I wrapped an arm around my waist. Spencer knelt down beside the chair, offering his reassuring presence.

"I panicked, of course." Mom went on. "I searched everywhere for him. His stroller was outside the gift shop, empty."

Her voice was shaky, and I knew it had to have been absolutely terrifying. I was petrified, and I was hearing about it after the fact.

"I started yelling for help. The security guards came. The employees came. People who were inside started helping me look for him."

"Where was he?" I demanded. The suspense was literally going to kill me.

"One of the guards found him near the exit of the building. It was two flights of stairs up from where he and I were." She sounded confused and upset all at once.

I blew out a shaky breath. "You're sure he isn't hurt?"

"Of course not, honey. I checked him over."

"Okay, I'm coming home right now."

She didn't argue because she knew it was a losing fight.

"Elle," she said right before I could disconnect the phone.

"Yeah?"

"There's something else."

"What?" I said, wishing she would just say it and get it over with.

"There was a note in his pocket. I found it when I was checking him over for injuries."

I glanced at Spencer, feeling all the blood drain from my face. "What did it say?" I asked.

"It was just two words: Hurry up."

I closed my eyes.

"Do you know what that means?" Mom asked.

Oh, I knew what it meant. It meant my time was running out.

I swallowed past the giant rock in my throat and closed my eyes. I felt Walsh's stare bore into me, and I knew what he was silently telling me.

I had to lie.

"No, Mom," I said, my voice hoarse. "I have no idea what it could mean."

"So odd," Mom said. She didn't question me at all.

Not like the people here. The people I was allowed to tell the truth. They didn't believe me. Mom would. Only I wasn't allowed to tell her. I wasn't allowed to have her support.

Like intense acid reflux, anger burned through my chest and up my esophagus. This had to stop.

"I'll see you soon," I said and then disconnected the phone.

I glanced up at Walsh, my eyes hard. "Tell me what you know."

I saw the excuse forming in his eyes, the half explanation he was going to try and spoon-feed me and expect me to accept.

Yeah, no.

I stood up from the chair. I didn't care I wasn't an impressive, intimidating size. It didn't matter. I was a mother. A mother whose child was being threatened. That alone could match the strength and size of a giant.

"You want to think I'm guilty?" I spat. "Fine." Walsh's eyes widened. "You don't want me to cook anything. No problem. You want to fire me when all this is over? That's fine, too. But," I said, hard, staring him down. "You will not keep this from me. You will not tell me only what you want me to know. My son is being threatened, and I expect you to be one hundred percent honest with me. So help me God, if you don't, I'll go to the press."

"I'll throw you in jail," Walsh countered, clearly not liking my ultimatum.

Spencer stepped up beside me.

"You won't," I said. "Because then your bait will be off the table."

Walsh studied me for long moments. I was aware of Spencer standing by, ready to jump to my defense.

But I didn't need him to defend me. I could defend myself.

Walsh sighed and slapped a folder onto his desk. "Our guys apprehended the kid who took Jack. They left him by a security guard and then made sure he was found. Jack never would have made it out of that building without being intercepted."

I crossed my arms over my chest, incredulous. "You mean to tell me your guys *watched* my son be taken from his grandmother and they didn't do anything until he was two stories up?"

"Our presence needs to stay hidden," Walsh retorted.

"My son's life is at risk!" I yelled.

Spencer dropped an arm over my shoulders, and I stiffened. "What happened, Walsh?" he asked.

"We have the kid in custody. Our guys took him immediately, then hung around to make sure Jack was safe. He's being questioned now."

"So you have the man plotting against the president?" I asked.

Walsh shook his head. "No, this is some kid. Barely eighteen. He says he was paid to play a prank."

"Kidnapping is not a prank," Spencer growled.

"Kid says he never planned to leave the building with Jack. He says he was paid to just walk the kid around, give the grandma a little scare."

"Who in the hell would agree to that!" I burst out.

"An idiot," Walsh said, pinching the bridge of his nose. "We're going to throw the book at him."

I snorted. No punishment would be good enough.

"Who hired him?" Spencer asked. I could practically hear the wheels turning in his head.

"We're trying to get the information out of him now. He doesn't seem to know very much."

I laughed hollowly. "I'm going home," I declared, stepping away from Spencer. "I don't care if it's not my normal time."

Walsh nodded. "There is something we need to discuss first."

"What?" I asked, desperate to get out of here.

"I think we need to consider a change in plans."

Spencer nodded like he already knew what Walsh was going to say.

"What kind of change?" I asked.

"I think it's time we send Jack away."

13

They were toying with me.

Preying on my weakest spot.

The stunt at the aquarium proved they were getting anxious and tired of waiting. They told me to do what they wanted quickly, and I hadn't.

My son paid the price.

I had only one choice.

I had to send Jack away.

I didn't want to. It was the last thing on Earth I wanted, but his life was more important than my wants. I'd never been away from him for more than one night, and the thought of it literally gave me hives.

I told myself to get over it, that I could bring him back the minute—no, the second—this was over.

There was only one problem.

I didn't know where to send him.

It seemed like sending him to visit family or close friends was the obvious answer, but it wouldn't necessarily hide him. He needed to go where no one would look, where no one would even think to look.

The Secret Service, I think, finally saw the situation for what it was: me being threatened and blackmailed to do something I would never do. The atmosphere in the office where we sat was subdued, and the faint odor of suspicion that seemed to waft off all of them (except Spencer) was gone.

They were currently suggesting where to send Jack and my mother. I didn't like any of their places.

"I know somewhere," Spencer said, his expression thoughtful.

"Where?" I asked.

He shook his head. "It would be better if you didn't know."

I made a strangled sound. "You expect me to send my mother and my son away for safety and *not* know where they will be?" He was crazy.

Spencer speared me with somber amber-colored eyes. "Do you trust me?"

I took my time answering because this was a moment when I needed to be one hundred percent certain. His gaze never wavered; the sincerity in his face never slipped.

The thing was I didn't really need time to come up with the answer to his question. I knew it immediately. What I needed time for was actually admitting the truth out loud.

"Yes," I said finally.

He smiled deeply, two lickable dimples appearing in his cheeks. "They will be safe. I promise you."

"Okay."

Spencer looked at Walsh. "I'll set it up."

Walsh regarded Spencer for a moment. "Yeah. Set it up."

Spencer stood. "I guess this means since I'm needed here, my *assignment* tonight is going to be covered by someone else?"

Walsh cleared his throat and glanced at me.

Apparently, the assignment and reason Spence couldn't be around tonight was a busy job to keep him away from me.

I gave Walsh a sweet smile.

"Fine," he muttered. He was defeated and he knew it.

Spencer jolted forward, pressing a swift, hard kiss to my mouth before rushing from the room with his phone in hand to presumably make the arrangements.

I pressed my lips together as he went, trying to hold on to the feeling of him on my skin just a little longer. Every eye in the room focused on me.

I lifted my chin and stared back, almost daring them to say something. Gazes averted almost immediately.

I hurried to scoop everything back into my bag, leaving it in a tangled heap at the bottom. I was anxious to get to my mom's and see Jack. I wanted to hold him. Only then would everything in my world be right.

Seconds later, Spence came in. "They can leave this afternoon."

"Are you sure about this?" I asked, worrying all over again. I hadn't expected him to leave so soon.

"Getting Jack out of here is the best thing," Spencer said. "You will be able to think more clearly without worrying about him, and we can all move around a little more freely without having to worry about his safety. We can get this case solved quicker."

Well, I was all for ending this nightmare as quick as possible.

"Okay."

"I need details, Waller," Robert barked.

"Of course, sir." He inclined his head.

"I'm going home," I announced.

No one tried to stop me, and I left before they changed their mind, escaping out into the hallway.

"Bring your mom and Jack to the Smithsonian in two hours," Spencer said, coming up behind me. "Pack light. Don't draw attention with bags. Make it look like a fun afternoon. Wait near the bathroom by the back entrance. I'll find you," he said, taking my arm gently, and looked at me.

I glanced around, noting we were alone. "Are you sure about this?" I asked, keeping my voice low.

"Yeah, I am." He reached up to tuck a strand of hair behind my ear.

I nodded. "Okay, then."

Spencer leaned down. I thought he was going to kiss me. He did, just in an unexpected place. His lips were soft and warm against my forehead when he brushed them there. Then he dropped another one in the same spot. I gripped his biceps, preventing him from pulling back so fast, and tilted back my head so it fell against the wall.

"I'm sorry," he murmured.

"For what?" I said, thinking he was going to apologize for what happened with Jack.

"For taking this long to do something about the way I feel about you."

My breath caught. "Spence," I whispered.

"I know," he said softly. "My timing sucks. Just know that once this is over and you guys are safe…" His voice trailed off and he kissed my temple. "I'm pursuing you, Elle. And I always —*always*—get what I want."

A little shiver raced up my spine and a tiny noise escaped the back of my throat. I felt his smile against my forehead.

"I'll see you in a bit," he said, releasing me, and gently steered me toward the stairs.

I walked away in a daze, totally turned on by his words. Being pursued by Spencer was going to be thoroughly exciting.

"Elle?"

I turned when he called out to me.

"Be careful," he said. It was a small reminder that my life was filled with very big problems.

Problems that needed solving immediately.

14

How did you explain to your mother that you were sending her and your son away because you were being threatened and blackmailed by unknown men to kill the president of the United States?

You didn't.

You lied.

Well, sort of.

Truth was I wasn't a good liar. She would smell it from a mile away, and the next thing I knew, I would be blubbering the complete truth to her and putting them in even more danger.

It was the power of the "mom look." Sometimes I practiced it in the mirror so I could use it on Jack, but it was elusive. I was no good at it.

The best lies are seeded in truth. At least that's what I heard on TV, so I decided to go with that theory.

"There's a breech in security at work," I told her as I cradled Jack on the couch. I just couldn't seem to put him down since I'd arrived at Mom's house. "A lot of White House information—personal information—

about the employees was taken. The security team there isn't certain what kind of threat this poses, but it's making me extremely nervous."

Mom's eyes were wide and concerned. "You think that's what today at the aquarium was about?"

"I don't know." I lied and pushed on. "But I've arranged for you and Jack to go somewhere and stay for a while."

"And leave you behind?"

"Yes. So no one will get suspicious. Routine as normal, work as normal."

"Elle." I knew that tone. She was going to argue. She was going to shoot down this idea.

I held up my hand. "Mom, please. This is for Jack's safety. Don't you want your grandson to be safe?"

He face blanched. I had her. She couldn't argue with me about Jack, especially not after earlier today. "Where will we go?"

"It's best if you just go there, see for yourself." I waited for her to pick up on the fact I had no clue myself, but for once, she didn't seem to notice.

"How long?"

"I'm not really sure," I replied truthfully. "Hopefully, only a handful of days."

She studied me for a long time. I tried to avoid her gaze as much as I could, instead focusing on Jack and tickling his belly. Gah, his little laugh was the best sound on Earth.

I wasn't sure what I was going to say if she refused or demanded more information. I couldn't tell her the truth.

"I'll go pack a bag," she finally said.

My shoulders slumped in relief. "Something very small and unassuming," I called after her. Her footsteps faltered but then continued on.

I went through Jack's diaper bag. He had two changes of clothes, some diapers, and a couple little containers of snacks and some juice boxes. He would be fine until they got where they were going. I prayed it was somewhere they could get some groceries and necessary items. My throat grew thick just thinking about saying good-bye to him and watching him leave without me knowing where he was going.

His little hands fisted in my hair and tugged on the ends, and I smiled, looking down at him. I ran my fingers over his light-brown, feather-soft hair and round, chubby cheeks. His lips were pink and his eyes were hazel with green flecks near the center. He was normal size for his age, but to me he was small. He probably always would be because he was my baby.

He was wearing a blue romper with sailboats on the front and little blue Nikes that I couldn't resist when I saw them in the store window. He grinned up at me, showing off some of the tiny teeth in his mouth. I kissed him on the head, holding him against me, but he didn't want anything to do with it. He wiggled until I put him down, and he went over to the corner where there was a big basket of toys.

Mom came back into the room, carrying an oversized tote bag that just looked like a large purse. I didn't think it would draw too much attention if anyone was watching.

Please let no one be watching.

I glanced at the clock. It wasn't long until we had to meet Spencer. I took a deep breath and tried to bury the worst of my anxiety. After I got to my feet and announced we needed to go, Mom took hold of my arms and looked directly into my eyes.

"Maybe once Jack and I get home, you can tell me what's really going on."

My lower lip wobbled. I nodded but didn't say anything else. She pulled me into a hug, and all I could think about was how horrible of a liar I was and that I was thankful she didn't press me for the details I couldn't give.

When she pulled back, she gave me a watery smile. "Don't you worry about Jack," she said. "I promise I will keep him safe."

"I know you will," I whispered and slung the diaper bag over my shoulder and went to retrieve Jack.

The cab ride to the Smithsonian was quiet, and all I could think about was Spencer and what kind of arrangements he was making for my family.

The inside of the museum was surprisingly busy for the afternoon on a weekday. Didn't people work? Of course, D.C. was always filled with tourists, and I guess today was no exception. We didn't rush through the museum to get to the bathroom near the back. Instead, we wandered through the first floor, looking at the exhibits. Jack liked the dinosaurs and the giant wooly mammoth on display.

My stomach knotted the closer we got to the back. I didn't tell Mom we were meeting anyone. I didn't tell her anything. I just hoped she didn't ask too many questions when Spencer showed up.

"I need to use the restroom," I said, hoisting Jack up into my arms when we arrived at the bathroom.

"I'll wait right here," Mom said. She didn't reach for Jack, and I was glad because I wanted to hold him while I had the chance.

I went in the busy bathroom and swashed my hands and pretended to check my makeup. I didn't really have to pee. I just wanted an excuse to be near the bathroom. When I stalled all I could, I carried Jack out into the hallway where people were shuffling all around. Mom was where I left her. She hadn't moved.

As soon as I stepped in place beside her, Spencer appeared.

"Ladies," he said, inclining his head at us. Both his hands were clasped behind him.

Mom looked up, her eyes widening just a bit.

"Mom, this is Spencer." I began. "He—um…"

"I'll be driving you," he said smoothly.

Mom glanced at me, and I nodded. "You can trust him."

Jack's eyes were fastened on Spencer. It was impossible not to see the way they lit up.

"Jack, my man," Spencer said, smiling. "How are ya?"

Jack smiled and held his arms out for Spencer.

My mother stared at me with an incredulous look on her face.

"Jack likes him," I muttered quietly.

"I have something for you, Jack," Spencer said, withdrawing his arms from behind his back to reveal a large green-colored sea turtle with large flippers.

"That's the turtle from the aquarium," Mom said as Jack shrieked. His little arms changed direction from Spencer and toward the turtle.

Spencer smiled and handed it over to him. Jack hugged it against his little body and tears sprang into my eyes for like the fiftieth time that day.

Jack held it out to me. "Look!"

"I love it!" I said, trying not to cry.

Jack held his arms out for Spencer again.

Spencer glanced at me, silently asking for permission. I nodded.

Jack fit into Spencer's arms with ease, him and the giant turtle. Jack grinned up at Spencer and kept his eyes trained on him like he was in awe. "What's up, little man?" Spencer asked him.

Jack held out the turtle and Spencer made the appropriate sounds of admiration.

It actually kind of caused my heart to ache seeing them together. It's what Jack should have had. That is if his biological father hadn't been a complete asshole.

"Jack," I said, my voice breaking a little. "Say thank you."

"'Sank you," he said.

"Anytime, buddy," Spencer said, shifting the little boy just a little closer in his arms.

I reached out for him, but he ducked his face into Spence's neck, wanting to stay where he was. This look crossed behind Spencer's eyes; I couldn't really place it. But it sure did look like he was content to hold my son.

"We should probably go," Spencer said after a few seconds.

Mom looked between the two of us with a calculating look in her eye. I knew when she got back, I was going to have to explain a lot more than just why I was really sending her away.

Goody.

We all walked quietly toward the back entrance. It wasn't really for guests, but for employees, but Spencer didn't seem to care. Out the glass of the door, I saw a large black 4x4 truck waiting nearby, and I glanced up at him.

He nodded.

"The car seat." I gasped.

"I took care of it," Spencer said, running a palm over the back of my head.

"Come here, bud," I said, taking Jack into my arms. "Give Mommy a kiss."

Jack gave me a sloppy two-year-old kiss and made me smile. "You have fun with Nana," I said. "I'll miss you." I couldn't help the choked-up tone of my voice.

"He's going to be fine," Spencer said, his voice totally confident.

I glanced at my mom. She nodded and gave me a one-armed hug. "Call if you can," she said into my ear.

Before I was ready, Spencer took Jack (who went willingly) into his arms and said, "Wait a little bit before you leave."

I nodded, looking at Jack.

They left through the side door moments later, and my son, looking totally content in Spencer's arms, waved at me over his shoulder. I waved back, then turned away, not wanting him to see me cry.

I hated the men who were threatening me like this. They were robbing me of time with my son and my feeling of safety. From here on out, I was going to focus on finding them and on making them pay.

15

It's funny how things seemed worse in the dark. They seemed scarier, too.

It had been hours since I said good-bye to Jack and my mom. Hours that I wondered where they were and if they were safe. I hoped I would get a call from Spencer or even Mr. Walsh to tell me they were okay.

But no call came.

The hour drew later and the sky outside turned black, giving me an even greater ominous feeling.

I stared out the window again and again, trying to figure out where the unmarked car was the Secret Service put on my house. I never saw it. I never even saw a hint of protection out there.

What if they were gone? What if they decided if I was dead, the threat to the president was as well?

But it wouldn't be. Those masked men would just find someone else to try and force. They were angry I hadn't done what they wanted. They were anxious and annoyed with me. How much longer could I do nothing until they came for me? For Jack?

Who could it be? Who could want the president dead? Who would gain the most from it? I had no idea. I didn't think like a killer or a politician. I thought like a chef. I thought in cups and spoons, in chocolate and herbs.

My stomach rumbled violently. I was beyond starving. Since I wouldn't be getting any sleep tonight, I might as well eat. Eating was better than staring out the window, looking for a person I would never see.

In the kitchen, I looked inside the fridge, but nothing appealed to me. The apples, the vegetables, the salad and chicken… nothing. I didn't feel like cooking either.

I opened the freezer and saw the large container of Rocky Road ice cream. Bingo. I pulled it out, then reached back in the fridge for the container of hot fudge and the whipped cream. Sugar made everything better.

I reached up into the cabinet for a large bowl and turned, stopping in my tracks.

The handle on the back door was jiggling, like someone was trying to get in. My grip around the bowl tightened. If worse came to worse, I could clobber them with it and hope it gave me time to run.

I glanced at my cell lying right there on the counter and wondered if I should call the police or Mr. Walsh.

I didn't have time to do either because the door swung open. A dark figure stepped in and quickly shut the door behind him. The man was wearing jeans and a dark hooded sweatshirt. When he turned abruptly and pushed the hood off his head, he revealed familiar dirty-blond hair.

I gasped. "Spencer!"

"Hey," he said, keeping his voice low. "Sorry to just let myself in. I didn't have time to knock and wait for you to answer."

"You scared the shit out of me," I said, setting the bowl on the counter.

"I'm sorry, darlin'."

"You could have called," I accused.

"I don't know who's listening," he replied, not angry at my accusation.

My shoulders slumped. He was right. When it came to my son, then I would rather be scared than have any information about his whereabouts leak.

"How's Jack?" I asked, desperate for any kind of news.

He strode across the room in two long strides and pulled me against his chest. He was warm and the steady beat of his heart made me believe everything was okay. "He's good," he said, a smile in his tone. "That boy is something else."

I pulled back to look at him. "He likes you."

"I like him, too," he said fondly as he scrolled through his phone. He extended the screen to me, holding out a picture that he must have taken of Jack.

He was smiling and still clutching the turtle Spencer gave him. He didn't seem scared at all, and there were trees and flowers in the background of wherever he was.

"He's okay?" I said, relief making me weepy.

"Yes. I promise."

"I've been worried," I confessed.

"I know."

"I was thinking," I said, changing the subject. "The person from the aquarium, the one that said he was paid to take Jack? We should get a sketch artist to do a drawing, maybe whoever hired him is the person who wants to kill the president."

He smiled. "Already on it. The artist has been with him this evening."

"Oh, good."

"Everything that is humanly possible to put an end to this is being done." He reassured me, his eyes automatically going around the room. He smiled when he saw the ice cream.

"You want some?" I asked.

"Got any cookies?" he asked.

I rolled my eyes. "No."

He debated.

"Is that a yes or a no?" I asked.

"Does a horse have a tail?"

I assumed that meant yes, so I went to get another bowl.

"How did you get in here?" I asked. "What if someone saw you?"

He scoffed. "I'm a Secret Service agent. Before that, I was military. No one saw me."

"A ninja with lots of training," I said, looking up from my task. "Good with kids, attractive, sexy car." I continued to list. "How is it you're single?"

He leaned across the counter and gave me a penetrating stare. "I'm a lot sexier than my car."

I smiled. "Maybe."

He took the spoon, which was covered in ice cream, and set it aside. Grasping my hand, he pulled me around the island, towing me up against his chest. "You know it."

"Hmmm." I pretended to debate.

"Do you question my sexiness?" he asked, lifting an eyebrow. At the same time, he reached for the hem of the T-shirt I put on after I got home.

"Maybe you should prove it," I purred.

What the hell was I doing? Getting involved with a man was not in the plans for me. Getting involved with one during a time when my life was a complete shit storm was even worse. 'Course, at the moment, I couldn't think of anything I'd rather do than feel his hands on me. Jack was safe; he was out of immediate danger. My mother was safe. The police were working with a witness and a sketch artist.

There really was nowhere I needed to be. Except right here in his arms.

"Darlin'," he drawled, sending tingles of excitement shooting through my lower body. "When I'm done with you, there won't be a single doubt in your mind."

I shrieked a little when he grabbed me around the waist and spun me off my feet. My bottom hit the island, and he stepped between my knees. His muscled arm wrapped around the small of my back, and he pulled, jerking me against him, and my core brushed up against the jeans he was wearing.

He was already hard. The front of his crotch strained against the jeans and pushed against me urgently.

It had been so long since I'd had sex that a groan ripped out of my throat. He grinned, looking rather smug, and swooped down, taking my lips. His kiss seared me to the very core. His lips were urgent and demanding. They were rough and enticing. There was a hint of stubble on his jaw and chin, and it rasped against my skin as he moved across my lips. The sensation was maddening.

My hands gripped the sides of his hips, flexing tightly and pulling him closer. I wrapped my legs around his hips just below his buttocks and returned his kiss with everything I had.

I wanted to make him feel the way he made me feel.

Out of control.

Horny.

On fire.

Ready to explode.

I ripped my mouth away from his, enjoying the sound of his heavy breathing, and scraped my teeth over his chin where the stubble was. Then I kissed down his neck and across his jaw, moving upward to capture his earlobe between my teeth.

He made a sound, and one of his hands flattened on the island behind me so he could throw all his weight onto it and lean into my kiss. I dragged my hands up the back of his neck and delved into his hair, taking fistfuls of it and guiding his mouth back down to mine.

His tongue delved into the depths of my mouth with ease, stroking around the inside of me, and caused shivers to rack my body. Spencer disconnected our mouths and pulled back, I watched him through desire-heavy eyes.

Spencer grabbed the hem of my T-shirt and yanked it up over my head and tossed it aside.

"Oh fuck," he said when he saw I wasn't wearing a bra. Both my nipples were rock hard, pulled into tight little pearls, standing at attention in the center of my full, perky breasts. I throbbed for his hands. I needed him to grab me, to massage the swollen flesh.

He dove down, sucking one into his mouth, and I arched my back upward, granting him all the access he wanted. Little sounds of pleasure filled the kitchen as I yanked at the shirt still keeping his skin from my hands.

With a little chuckle, he pulled back and his shirt joined mine.

I sighed just looking at him. His bronzed, toned body was on display for me for the first time. He had a long, narrow waist; it rippled with muscle and begged for my fingernails to scrape across it. His shoulders were so broad and strong it made me squeeze my thighs together around him.

My hands were greedy, and I reached for him. I wanted to touch every last part of him. I wanted to admire the rough and smooth contrast of his skin. I wanted to tangle my fingers in the golden chest hair that spanned his remarkable chest.

On impulse, he grabbed me and lifted me off the counter. I tightened my legs around him, and with one hand, he yanked the shorts I was wearing down over my ass. The counter was cold against my bare bottom when he sat me back down. His hands ripped the clothing the rest of the way off, and then I was totally naked before him.

His lips fastened on mine again as he pushed me down so I was lying across the island, completely on display for him. He didn't kiss me long enough, but pulled back and picked up the can of whipped cream right beside my head.

"What are you doing?" I asked, my voice thick to my own ears.

Spencer's smile was wicked as he yanked the top off with his teeth and spit it on the floor. Then he shook the can and held it upside down, angling right above my breast.

The sound of whipped cream dispensing filled the kitchen as the cold, light topping landed on my skin. He twirled it around, covering both my nipples with it and then drawing a trail down the center of my belly all the way down to my crotch.

My knees trembled with excitement when he grabbed up the chocolate sauce and tossed the lid over his shoulder. He watched me suggestively as two of his fingers dipped into the sinfully sweet sauce and then lifted out, smearing it across my chest.

He stared right into my eyes when he licked off what was left on his fingers and then climbed up to straddle me on the counter.

A growling sound erupted from somewhere deep in his chest as he began to lick the dessert off me. Long, hungry strokes of his tongue lapped up the sweet stuff, and he was *very* thorough. My nipples began to ache because they were so hard, and I moaned, grabbing at one and giving it a squeeze.

"What's the matter, darlin'?" he drawled in between licking down my stomach.

I made an impatient sound and he chuckled. As he continued lower, one of his wide palms came up and settled over my breast and squeezed. Relief washed through me. I was wound so tight I was going to snap at any second.

Spencer withdrew his hand to grab my legs and drape them over his shoulders, positioning himself at my entrance. My eyes slid closed when his tongue made contact.

It was so good. He knew exactly where to lick, exactly where to suck, and precisely where to touch. His fingers teased my swollen clit as his tongue speared my wet opening, causing me to arch up off the table.

One of his fingers slid inside me, and I moaned. He shifted up so he could stare down at me. "You're so fucking tight," he ground out.

"It's been a long time." I gasped as his finger moved inside me, tentatively stretching out my inner walls.

"Good," he growled.

"Spencer," I whimpered, wanting far more that just his finger. I pushed up onto my elbow and stared into his dark, honey eyes. They practically smoldered with freaking sexual power.

He stood up and slowly withdrew the finger inside me. Then, keeping hold of my gaze, he put it in his mouth and licked off every last bit of me.

The bottom of my stomach completely fell out. It was hard to breathe. My body didn't want to do anything accept feel him inside me.

I looked down for his hard cock, ready to grab it. Ready to feel it slide into me.

He was still wearing jeans.

Disappointment was like a knife cutting deep. I sat up the rest of the way, swaying slightly. He grabbed hold of my waist as I attacked the button and zipper on his jeans.

I wished I had the patience to kiss his body, to work my tongue all over him. But I didn't. All I could think about was getting him inside me.

Spencer pushed down his boxers and jeans, his thick rod shooting out between us, on proud display. I reached for it, wrapping my hand around the base and giving it a gentle squeeze. My hand dragged upward, pulling at the throbbing flesh, working him. I wanted him as desperate as me. I wanted him to take me hard, fast, and deep.

His head rolled back on his shoulders, a low moan filling the room. I smiled and began sliding my hand up and down his shaft with a quicker pace. I enjoyed the way he throbbed in my hand, like he was anxious for more.

I was about to lean down and take him into my mouth when he pushed me back and yanked my legs toward him. My ass was off the island completely now, but I was in no danger of falling. My legs wound around the narrow part of his waist and the firm tip of his cock pressed against my opening.

"Yes," I whispered.

He thrust forward, invading my body, immediately stretching out my tight insides with one single stroke. My mouth fell open, but no sound came out.

He gave me exactly what I wanted, pounding into me with the kind of fervor that caused me to moan over and over again. I couldn't see anything because I was blinded by passion. I couldn't feel anything but his solid rod spearing me again and again.

I rocked against him, wanting him as deep as he could possibly go. The veins in his biceps stood out with the bulging of his muscles, and the sound of our bodies slapping together was sweet music.

"Spencer," I whimpered as my body spiraled closer and closer to release. It was such a powerful feeling that it made me slightly nervous.

"I'm right there with you, baby," he murmured, his voice strained.

My back was jerked up off the counter. He pulled me into a sitting position and wrapped his arms around my waist, pulling me in to him farther, driving his length in deeper.

His eyes found mine and a look passed between us, the kind of look I would never in my entire life forget. It went deeper than his cock ever could.

He caught my lips in a gentle kiss. It was a direct contrast to the way in which he was making love to me. Our lips fused together as a shudder moved through him. With one last hard thrust, he began to come, his hot seed spraying my inner walls, and I moaned.

Spencer swallowed every sound that resulted in the orgasm ripping through my body, and he kissed me until my limbs went slack and I collapsed, completely spent, against him.

Somehow, he supported both our weight as our breathing returned to normal.

"Shit, Elle," he swore against my hair. "I knew you were hot, but that was…"

I giggled.

"That was fucking shattering."

I couldn't agree more.

Still totally boneless, he lifted me off the island and carried me into the living room, where he collapsed on the couch, not once separating our bodies.

With his hands cupping my hips, he kissed me again. He kissed me like he hadn't just been all over my body, like this was his first taste of me. I shifted my body, rolling my hips over him, and felt his cock stir to life.

He pulled back and looked at me, surprise flickering in his gaze.

"Again?" I said, rocking against him.

"Clearly, I'm up for it," he drawled.

This time I rode him, pressing his hard body into the cushions of my couch and watching all the expressions of satisfaction that came over his face. I moved slower this time, taking the opportunity to feel his body, to get to know it. He seemed all too happy to lie back and let me touch him. His body was my own personal playground.

Eventually, the playtime became too much and both our bodies needed more. Spencer pulled me close, bringing our bare chests together as I ground down on his lap.

I called out his name when release rippled through me, and he held me even tighter.

When we were done, my legs felt rubbery and the center of my body felt swollen, but it was a pleasurable feeling. I don't think I'd ever been so satisfied in my entire life.

In the kitchen, I slid his T-shirt over my body because it was the first one I saw. But it was also because I wanted to wear it.

I stood gazing down at the melting ice cream, smears of chocolate, and whipped cream all over the island. I would never look at this kitchen the same way again.

Solid arms encircled me from behind, and he nuzzled my ear.

"You made a mess," I said, rubbing a palm over his forearm.

He grunted, and I laughed.

My entire body felt sticky. "I need a shower."

"Me, too," he said, pulling me closer against him.

I shut my eyes and enjoyed the feeling of being held. It had been so long, and even then, it never felt this right.

"The bathroom is upstairs, first door on the left," I told him. "Go ahead up. I'll just take care of this and meet you in there."

He groaned and buried his face in the back of my hair. "You smell good."

"I probably smell like chocolate because someone made a giant sundae out of my body," I said, smiling.

"Best damn sundae I ever ate."

I spun in his arms and looped my own around his neck. "Really," I said. "Why are you single?"

The color of his eyes was incredible, and the intensity behind his direct stare had this way of taking over my entire being. "I've been focused on my career. In the Marines, I was too busy overseas and working to get serious with anyone, and then I signed on at the White House and I was too busy trying to establish myself there and to be taken seriously at a young age." He shrugged beneath my arms. "No one's ever made me want to make room in my life."

"I guess I can understand that." I felt a little pang that he didn't want to make room in his life for me. But it was for the best. I had Jack to think about. I wasn't about to let another man into his life—into my life— that would only walk out again.

He gazed at me seriously. "I want to make room for you, Elle."

I averted my gaze. He'd just said the words I wanted to hear, but now that they were out there, I wasn't sure I wanted them to be. All the reasons I just thought of were still there. I couldn't risk letting him in only to be hurt again.

"Spence," I said, lifting my face. He didn't let me speak. Instead, he kissed me. It was soft and sweet; he coaxed my lips open like gentle rays of the sun on a flower after a rainstorm. He didn't press me. He didn't demand. He merely kissed me until I offered more.

It stole away my heart.

When he finally pulled away, I dropped my forehead down onto his shoulder, pressing my mouth together and trying to control my shaking insides.

"Darlin'," he drawled, whispering in my ear. "I know you have to think about Jack. I know that boy comes first, and I understand it. Hell, I'm in awe of you."

I pulled back and looked at him questioningly.

"To have accomplished everything you have and be raising that boy all by yourself..." He shook his head. "I respect you for it. I'm damn proud of you."

I swallowed past the lump in my throat.

"I'm not trying to rush you into anything. I'm just saying I want you. I want to know everything about you, and if and when you decide it's okay, I'd like to know Jack, too."

My lips parted. "Most men don't want anything to do with another man's child."

"I'm not most men," he replied. "And Jack isn't some other man's child. He's *yours*."

Emotion welled up inside me, causing my chest to feel tight. I didn't know what to say. I was so overwhelmed.

He leaned down, hovering just above my lips, his eyes seeking something in mine. I closed the distance and kissed him, hoping he understood everything I was feeling.

"Go shower," he said when we broke apart. "I got this."

"You're sure?"

He reached around me and grabbed my ass. "I'm sure. Save me a spot under the spray."

I grinned. "'Kay."

I left him to clean up the mess from our "snack" and went into my bedroom to get some clean clothes to take into the bathroom with me. On my way out of my closet, clothes clutched in hand, an eerie feeling came over me.

I glanced over my shoulder at the window.

It was open.

It hadn't been before.

Spencer and I weren't alone in this house.

16

My clothes hit the ground soundlessly, and I looked around with a powerful sense of fear. I knew for an absolute fact that window had been shut.

And locked.

Since all this started, I was obsessed with checking and rechecking the windows and doors.

I stood stock still, listening for any kind of indication of where the intruder might be. The only thing I could hear was the sound of my own ragged breathing.

Flashbacks from the night they first invaded this home rendered me petrified, and all I could think about was getting the hell out.

Not taking another second to think about it, I crept toward the bedroom door and peaked out into the hallway. When I saw no one was there, I rushed to the stairs and crept down.

I heard a sound coming from somewhere behind me, and it was all I could do to not scream. Instead, my heart leapt into my throat, and I rushed down the stairs at warp speed, afraid to look behind me. I rounded the banister and shot forward, running toward the kitchen.

I collided with something hard and gasped.

Spencer grabbed my shoulders and looked into my eyes. "What's wrong?"

"There's someone in the house," I whispered.

His face grew angry and dark. My fear increased tenfold. What if Spencer got hurt?

Without another word, he wrapped his arm around my waist and lifted me off my feet, hauling me back into the kitchen. He grabbed his gun that was lying on the counter (the first time I'd noticed it since he'd arrived, but then again, I was busy) and put a finger up to his lips.

I rolled my eyes.

Did he really think he needed to tell me to be quiet?

He leaned down and spoke low in my ear. "Stay with me."

Wait a minute. Was he going *up* there? Shouldn't we be getting the hell out?

I grabbed hold of his hand and gave it a hard tug. He turned back, holding the gun at his side. I pointed to the door, motioning for us to use it.

He shook his head and held up the gun.

My eyes widened. Was he crazy?

A thump echoed from upstairs, and Spencer started to move. I could only rush after him, unwilling to leave him here alone.

The noise continued as we slowly went up the steps. Spencer kept his finger on the trigger and moved with purpose, using his body as a shield for mine. Whoever was up here seemed to be shut in the small third bedroom at the end of the hall.

I kept all of Jack's toys in there. Sort of like a playroom. Of course, Jack only ever dragged his toys out of there and into one of our bedrooms or downstairs, so maybe it was more of a storage room.

And now it was harboring a criminal.

As soon as we cleared the top step, both of us stood in the hall, staring at the door I never closed. Suddenly, the sound of high-pitched laughter rang out. I jumped, nearly having a freaking heart attack as this creepy-crawly feeling skittered over my nerves.

Hahahahah. Heehehehehe.

The sound echoed through the quiet house.

I knew it was one of Jack's toys, but it still scared the shit out of me. I felt my arms shaking and tried to ignore it.

The laughter stopped.

Spencer motioned toward the door and for me to stay where I was. I wrapped my arms around my middle as he crept toward the door, gun drawn and muscles bunched.

He reached out to turn the handle.

I held my breath.

The metal of the round doorknob rattled in his hand as Spencer tried to open the door. He glanced at me with raised eyebrows. I shook my head. I never locked that door. Why would I?

Another thump and more laughter went off from inside.

Hahahahah. Heehehehehe.

I was so throwing that toy in the trash later.

I had one of those key things that opened all the doors in this house. It was like a piece of straight metal with a handle on the end that one could insert into the lock and pop it out to open the door.

I rushed into my room and pulled open my top dresser drawer. After a second of fishing around, my hand closed around it and I rushed back into the hallway and held it up.

Spencer nodded and held up his hand. I tossed it to him and he snatched it out of the air.

Keeping hold of his gun, he moved forward to pop the lock.

This odd feeling, like being watched or of something not being right, came over me. I turned to stare back into my room.

Something was off…

I walked back into the room, staring at everything, trying to understand exactly what felt wrong.

A dark figure came out of nowhere, appearing soundlessly behind me. I didn't have time to react, to do anything at all. He slapped a hand with a rag over my face and jabbed me in the kidney with his fist.

I hunched over in pain as he dragged me backward into my closet.

Out in the hall, I heard the lock pop and Spencer burst into the other room.

A man wearing a black ski mask and dark clothing shoved me against the wall, pinning me by the throat. The rag he held over my face and mouth was doused in some kind of chemical, and it smelled incredibly sweet.

"This is your last warning, bitch," the intruder growled. "If he's not dead by the night of the dignitary dinner, then you will be."

My brain became fuzzy, overruling the intense fear in my body. I couldn't struggle. I couldn't fight back. All my air supply was cut off, my lungs were seizing, and the pain in my throat radiated over my entire body.

Yet, I felt somehow detached.

Unfocused.

Far away.

"You understand?" the man growled, tightening his grip.

From somewhere far away, I heard a cat hiss and meow.

I didn't have a cat.

A gun went off.

The man holding me chuckled. Then he shoved his face so close to mine that I wanted to recoil, but I was unable. His breath was hot on my ear when he whispered, "That new man of yours is a real pussy hater. Better be careful."

He pulled the rag and his violent grip away. I sagged to the floor, falling into a heap among my hanging dresses and shirts.

Spencer yelled my name, and I heard a scuffle and commotion.

Another shot was fired.

Glass shattered.

The lights went out.

17

"Why won't she wake up?"

The urgent tone of the deep voice intruded upon the darkness claiming me. It was unbelievably thick, and I began to panic that I wouldn't be able to get free.

"He used chloroform on her. You know that shit knocks people out," another voice replied.

"He was right under my fucking nose," he growled. "He fucking got her, and I was standing right here."

"This isn't your fault, Waller."

"I'm going to fucking kill him," he swore.

I wanted to call out to Spencer, to tell him I was okay. The pure rage and fear in his voice cut through the darkness and attached itself around me. Every word he spoke towed me further to the surface.

"Do I need to remove you from this investigation?" the man responded. "I can put you on another detail until this is over."

I felt the deadly calm radiate around the room. "Try," Spence growled. "I won't listen."

"You would risk your entire career for this perp?" the man asked. I think it was Walsh.

"Not for him," Spencer rebuked. "For her."

I tried to force my eyelids open. I wanted to shout that I was here, and I didn't want him sacrificing anything for me.

"Are you in love with her?" Walsh asked, his voice quiet.

Everything inside me stilled. I stopped struggling against the sludge holding me under. The only thing I could focus on was that question and the answer Spencer would give.

Seconds ticked by.

"*Fuck*," he swore. The pure emotion behind his favorite word speared me. I felt him move closer, felt him staring down at me. "She totally snuck up on me," he whispered.

And just like that, I shoved through the heaviness. I wanted so badly to look into Spencer's amber gaze.

He loved me.

I blinked my eyes open. It took long moments to focus, and when I finally did, all I saw was Spence. His face was drawn. His hair was a wreck, and his jaw was unshaven. He wasn't wearing a shirt, and I realized it was because I was wearing it. All he had on was a pair of jeans, and he was looking across the room.

Walsh sighed heavily. "I can't say I'm surprised. You spend more time in the kitchen than any agent should."

"Hey," Spencer said, his voice growing hard. "I do my job."

"Yes, you do. And you're good at it."

"If you take me off this case, I'll go rogue." Spencer warned.

My voice scraped from my sore throat. "No."

He was right there instantly, bending over me, his eyes filled with concern. "Elle?"

I smiled groggily. "Hey…"

He let out a string of inappropriate cuss words and then dropped on the edge of the bed, making my body slide against his hip when the mattress dipped. "How are you feeling?"

"Kind of fuzzy," I said.

His hands brushed at my hair, sweeping it back from my face. "It'll wear off."

I nodded. "Jack?"

"He's fine, darlin'."

"What happened?" I asked.

"We were hoping you could tell us," Walsh said from across the room.

I frowned.

"Take your time," Spencer said.

I moved to sit up and he wrapped his arm beneath me and helped. We were in my bedroom, at my house. I glanced around as the fog lifted from my brain.

I remembered the man in the house…

The window was still open and the pane above the bottom one was shattered. I remembered the sound of the gun going off.

I gasped and grabbed Spencer's arm. "Are you okay?"

"I'm fine." He assured me.

"The man that was here…" My eyes went to the closet, and everything that happened came back to me.

Crap. I wasn't wearing any pants.

I looked down, totally mortified. Blankets covered me to my waist. I breathed a sigh of relief and looked at Spencer. He winked.

Heat suffused me as I remembered what Spencer and I were doing before the man broke in again.

"Elle, what happened?" Walsh asked, stepping closer to the bed.

"Did you call the police?" I worried, not wanting any of this to hit the news. It would only anger whoever was behind this more.

"Of course not. The Secret Service is handling this for now," Walsh replied.

Spencer remained tightlipped, his jaw tight. I had the overwhelming urge to smooth my hand over his rough jaw and take away some of the edge from within his eyes. Our audience kept my hand in my lap.

I realized Walsh knew there was something between us, but he'd been privy to enough of our private moments for one night.

"Did I hear a cat?" I asked, distracting myself from thoughts of Spence.

"There was a cat in the room," Spencer said. "He locked it in there."

"Why on Earth would he do that?" I wondered.

"To distract me," Spencer muttered. "To get you alone."

"Spence," I said softly, reaching for his hand. I hated seeing him beat himself up this way.

He stood, gently rebuffing my hand, and paced the carpet.

"I heard gunshots." I remembered.

"I fired at the cat. It leapt at me and I just reacted."

"Did you kill it?" I worried.

He stopped pacing and looked at me. "You're worried about a cat?"

"It's a helpless animal."

Walsh and Spencer looked at me like I was insane.

I don't see what the big deal was. I mean, geez, a girl needed to know if a cat was shot and killed in her house.

"Well?" I demanded, not backing down from their looks.

"No, the cat's fine," Spencer muttered.

"And the window?" I asked, glancing at the shattered panes.

"I shot those out, too," Spencer muttered.

"It's not like you to miss a shot." Walsh grunted.

Spencer stiffened. "I wasn't looking at him. I was looking for Elle when I fired."

"So he got away?"

"Yes," Spencer growled. Then he came to my side. "I'm sorry. If I'd have shot him, this would be over."

"I don't think so," I said.

"He dragged you in the closet," Walsh said. "Did he speak to you?"

I nodded, my hand going up to my throat where the flesh felt swollen and sore. The fear of being pinned against the wall, of the life being choked out of me as I tried to suck in air only to get mouthfuls of chloroform instead, washed over me.

"You need to back off," Spencer growled, straightening to face Walsh.

Walsh's face grew dark, and I hurried to speak before the two men began to argue.

"It's fine. I need to tell you so we can figure out what to do next. The clock is ticking."

That got their attention.

"Did he threaten you?" Spencer asked murderously.

"No. We had tea," I snapped.

Then I sighed, guilt pummeling me. "I'm sorry." I sighed. "I'm just…"

"I know, baby," Spencer said softly, sitting down beside me again. "It's okay."

Walsh groaned.

"He dragged me in the closet." I began, fingering my bruised neck again. "And pinned me to the wall. My mouth was covered with that stuff so I couldn't call out, and it was so…. sickly sweet that it made me drowsy almost instantly."

"Go on," Walsh instructed.

"He told me if the president wasn't dead by the night of the dignitary's dinner, then he was going to kill me because I was of no use to him."

"Fuck," Spencer spat and jumped off the bed.

I really was going to have to speak to him about his foul mouth if he was going to be spending time with Jack.

That's when I knew.

I knew I wasn't going to be able to resist him. I wasn't going to be able to hold him at arm's length forever. As much as I didn't want a relationship with a man… I wanted Spencer more.

Even my subconscious was filled with thoughts of him and my son together.

"Elle?" Walsh said, drawing me out of my thoughts. "What else did he say?"

I glanced at Spencer, my cheeks heating. "Nothing important," I muttered.

"Everything is important," Walsh snapped.

Spencer stiffened.

"It's okay," I said. "After Spencer's gun went off, he said, 'That new man of yours is a real pussy hater. Better be careful.'"

"He's a fucking comedian," Spencer growled.

"What else?" Walsh pressed.

I shook my head. "That's all. We were only in there a moment. I think he was afraid Spencer would catch him."

"He should be," Spence muttered.

"He just threatened me, gave me a deadline, and then left."

Walsh and Spencer exchanged a long look. It was filled with meaning.

"It's an inside job," Spencer said.

Walsh nodded. "Yep."

"What!" I gasped, springing forward. Pain in my lower back made me wince and kept me from getting up. "How could you possibly know that?"

"He knows the White House is having a dignitary's dinner. That stuff doesn't make the news. The White House has too many events to be reported on. It has to be someone who has access to the calendar of events, someone on the inside."

"And now he knows you aren't here alone, Elle," Walsh said. "If he works at the White House, then I have no doubt he knows it's Spencer you are with."

"How could he know that?" I asked.

Walsh gave me a knowing look. "Everyone knows about you and Waller. We saw it coming months ago."

So everyone knew but me?

I thought of something else. "So if he knows about me and Spencer, then… he probably knows that I told him?"

"Maybe not," Spencer said. "He told you to be wary of me. Maybe he was trying to drive a wedge between us, keep you separated and alone."

"Like I would listen to a man who was trying to strangle me," I muttered.

My comment caused Spencer to stiffen and his jaw muscles to lock down. Probably not the best choice of words.

Good going, Elle.

"I think we should assume he thinks she told," Walsh said.

Panic assaulted me. I jumped up from the bed, swaying a little on my feet. "But what about Jack!" I demanded. "If he thinks I told, then he's going to go after my son!"

"He won't be able to find him," Spencer said, taking me by the shoulders and staring into my eyes. "Jack is safe."

I latched onto Spencer's face, trying to calm the brutal freak-out ripping through my insides. "Then he's going to kill me."

Spencer's fingers dug into my skin. "No. He won't."

"He already said he would. He said to kill the president by the night of the dinner or he would kill me."

Spencer jerked away from me, pacing the room again. Then he stopped mid-stride, his announcement shocking.

"Then I guess we're going to kill the president."

18

You could have heard a pin drop.

The silence filled the room, pressing in on all of us as we sat there and stared at Spencer.

Did he just suggest we *kill* the president of the United States?

Maybe he was overly tired.

Maybe he was too stressed out.

"You've lost your ever-lovin' mind!" Walsh roared, making me jump and disrupting the quiet.

Well, there was that.

But I wasn't about to jump on the bandwagon that Spencer had gone cuckoo. It wasn't possible. I needed him around too much.

"It's the perfect plan," Spencer said. His tone of voice suggested he could be talking about something as mundane as the weather.

I blinked.

"Once he's dead, the people behind this will get sloppy. We'll be able to catch them."

"And he won't come after me or Jack," I said.

Spencer's eyes cut to me and then away. I noted the hard set of his jaw before he forcefully relaxed it.

What did I say?

"There's just one problem with your plan, Waller," Walsh said. "I'll see you in jail before I let you off the commander in chief."

Spencer grunted. "Seriously? Give me some credit."

Walsh and I looked at each other.

"We aren't actually going to *kill* him, just make it look like we did." Spencer turned thoughtful. "It's the perfect excuse to get him out of harm's way anyway. We can send him into hiding."

"Do you know the kind of mass hysteria that will invite? The other countries who hate us will see it as a golden opportunity to strike," Walsh said, grim.

I felt all the hope leave my body. He was right. It couldn't work.

"Not if we played it right."

"What's the plan, Waller?" Walsh said. "Spit it out already! I haven't got all damn night."

"Put her back in the kitchen."

"This isn't about cookies," Walsh snapped.

"Let her get back to her daily routine at work. We kept this quiet at the White House. No one knew but a very limited few that she was at the center of a threat to the president. So she goes back to work. Business as usual. Whoever is on the inside will see it. They will be appeased. They will think she's going to do it."

"Keep talking," Walsh said, clearly liking Spencer's line of thought.

"And then she does it," Spencer said, like it was just that easy. "The president pretends to pass out. We cart him off into safety and let the news spread like wildfire through the White House that he's dead."

"What about the press?" I asked.

"We keep it contained in the White House for a couple days. Gag order the entire staff. Tell them we aren't announcing until we can get a statement, get the vice president briefed, yadda, yadda… You know, political stuff."

"It's a small window," Walsh muttered.

I wasn't sure what he meant by that.

"Yeah. It is. We won't be able to keep it quiet for long. But we already know the people behind this are anxious. They gave her a deadline. As soon as they think he's dead, they're going to do something to give themselves away."

"And then we'll get them," Walsh said, nodding his head.

Spencer looked smug. "And the president comes out of hiding and gets back to work."

"We'll go with it. Meeting in my office first thing tomorrow."

"Are we seriously doing this?" I asked, their rapid-fire plan and decision making was giving me a headache.

Or maybe it was the drugs I inhaled.

Walsh pinned me with a look. "Back to work in the morning. Back to cooking."

"Oh, you suddenly decided I'm not guilty?" I couldn't help the bitterness in my voice.

"I suddenly decided to give you a chance to prove you aren't," Walsh countered and walked toward the door.

I was glad to see him go.

Of course, the minute I thought that, he turned back around.

"You know it's not going to be so cut and dry," he said directly to Spencer.

He nodded tightly.

What did that mean? Why did the room suddenly feel ten degrees colder?

"Better enjoy tonight," Walsh said as he left the room and went down the stairs. "It's going to be a while before you get another one."

The sound of the front door latching echoed through the house.

"Spence," I whispered.

He was at my side in two seconds flat. Cool air brushed over my bare legs when he ripped the covers away and slid beneath them. The worn texture of his jeans rubbed against my legs, and I pushed myself against him, wishing I could get even closer.

"What a fucking mess," he muttered, stroking my hair. His harsh words were a direct contrast to the way he was behaving toward me.

I grabbed onto his forearms and held on, like I was on a rollercoaster and he was the safety bar.

"When I turned around and saw you weren't there," he whispered, "it was the worst feeling I've ever had."

"I'm sorry."

"What're you sorry for?" he rasped. "You didn't do anything, darlin'."

"You said to stay with you. I didn't listen."

"You're here with me now," he said, pulling back to look at me.

I didn't let go of him; my hands stayed firmly around his arms.

"I'm gonna stay this time." I promised. I hoped he understood the veiled meaning behind my words.

I'm yours.
Don't hurt me.
I think I'm falling for you.
He closed his eyes like the words were painful. When he reopened them, I noted the amber flame deep in their depths. "I'm gonna keep you." Spence accentuated the softly spoken words by tucking my hair behind my ear.

Those words affected me more deeply than if he'd said I love you.

I smiled because there was no way I could keep the giddy joy he just gave me inside.

"You're so beautiful," he whispered.

"Even with bruises, tangled hair, and bloodshot eyes?"

"Especially."

"I like a guy who's easy to impress." I smiled.

He chuckled and the sound was like a heating pad to all my aches and pains.

"Spence," I whispered again.

"Elle," he whispered back.

"Remind me," I prompted.

"Remind you of what?"

"Of what it's like to feel something other than scared to death. Of something other than physical pain."

"Baby, I'm sorry you hurt." He brushed his thumb across my bottom lip.

I leaned forward and kissed him. His lips parted and I slipped my tongue inside as he pulled me down so my entire body was on top of his. His hands slipped beneath the hem of his shirt I still wore and his fingers traced the line of my spine.

I nipped at his lower lip and sucked his tongue into my mouth. He gave me total control, lying back and letting me set the pace of the kiss. But it was hard to take control when I felt so out of control.

I wanted him to take over. I wanted to follow his lead, not because I was weak, but because every good warrior used a shield.

Spencer was my shield.

He seemed to sense my inner floundering and abruptly rolled, pinning me beneath him and covering me with his muscular frame. Before he kissed me, he drew back. "This okay?"

"Perfect."

He kissed me with a smile on his lips. I swallowed the feeling whole, wanting all the happiness I could taste. The hard ridge straining against his jeans pushed against me insistently, and I moaned.

How is it that I wanted him again already? I felt like he was touching me for the first time all over again. I loved the way he seemed to wrap around me, how when I was with him, all my fears and anxiety melted away

I reached between us, fingering the button on his jeans and opening them. His mouth left mine and trailed across my jaw and down to my neck. I spread my thighs eagerly, giving him more than enough room to settle between them.

God, the way he felt on top of me was incredible, and the way he supported most of his weight on his arms so he didn't hurt me.

I rubbed against him like his body was the beat to my favorite song. After several tries, I managed to get his jeans down enough for his erection to spring free. The smooth round head slid through my warm juices and made him shudder.

I smiled and raked my nails across his lower back, pressing him closer, inviting him in.

It only took one try for him to find the sweet spot, the entrance to the core of my body. Spencer slid right in, spearing me from the inside, and my legs flopped languidly against the bed.

He moved inside me, rocking back and forth. The action of his hips as he slid into me again and again was almost my undoing.

I gripped at his naked ass, pulling him even deeper.

"Closer," I urged.

I felt his arms slide up so his hands could grip the top edge of the mattress. The pressure of his added weight against me made me shiver. I buried my face into the side of his neck as he used the mattress as leverage to pull himself even deeper.

I moaned. Or maybe it was a growl. Holding himself that deeply, he began to make little rocking motions, the head of his cock throbbing against my walls.

Without thought, my teeth sank into his shoulder as an intense orgasm ripped through my body. I shuddered and trembled beneath him, little whimpers escaping the back of my throat as my teeth stayed firmly in his flesh.

In the middle of my explosion, his body stiffened and he released the mattress. Quickly, he slid both hands around my back and held me against him as I felt him pour every last drop of himself deep within my body.

When it was over, he still lay on top of me, breathing heavily. The shirt I was still wearing was stuck to me, and I felt sweat slick his broad back.

Finally, he leveraged himself up and looked down at me. Satisfaction was heavy in his stare. I gasped, noticing the teeth marks I'd left behind in his shoulder. "Did I hurt you?" I asked, brushing my fingers over the marks.

"Hell no," he drawled. "You can bite me anytime you want."

"Well, if you keep making love to me like that, I probably will."

He turned smug. "Is that an open invitation?" he asked, lowering down to kiss me. Then he kissed me again.

"You always do that," I whispered.

"Do what?"

"Kiss me twice. Never once."

"That's because one taste of you is never enough."

"It's an open invitation," I whispered, answering his earlier question. "One I hope you'll use very often."

"Just try and keep me away." He rolled to the side and we both lay there staring up at the ceiling. The normal sounds of nighttime drifted in through the window, sounding closer than usual. Then I remembered the window was busted.

"Are we safe here?" I asked, turning to look at the broken panes.

"I don't think he'll be back tonight," Spencer said.

"What about the window?" I asked.

"I can put something over it."

But the house would still be vulnerable. I would still feel watched. Would I ever feel safe in my house again?

Spencer rolled onto his side, propping his head up on his hand. "You're freaked out."

"Aren't you?"

"I'm a man. Men don't get freaked out."

I rolled my eyes.

He reached down and threaded his fingers through mine. "But I don't like seeing those bruises on your skin. I don't like seeing the shadows in your eyes."

Suddenly, I felt like crying. I missed Jack. I missed feeling safe in my own bed. I missed not having to worry about dying.

"Come on," he said, jumping up from the bed. His jeans slid down around his legs. It made me laugh. He grinned and yanked them back up, fastening the button.

"Where are we going?" I asked.

"Some place you'll be able to get some sleep."

I let him tug me to my feet. "Where is that?"

He smiled. "My place."

19

I couldn't help but be curious about the place Spencer called home. I already knew quite a bit about him, even though up until recently we spent most of our time flirting. You could learn a lot about a person in between flirting and cookie snatching.

He lived in an apartment not too far from the White House, on a busy street in D.C. (although almost all the streets in D.C. were busy). When he opened the door, I went in ahead of him, my eyes eagerly taking in the space. But it was dark. I couldn't really see much. So instead, I shuffled a little farther into the room, hoping I didn't trip and fall over something I couldn't see.

Spencer chuckled and reached around me to hit the light on the wall. I was momentarily distracted from the room as his arm brushed over me. I tipped my head back and smiled up at him. He leaned down and gave me a loud kiss that made me laugh.

"Wait a minute," he said when I pulled back. "I need another one."

I was totally charmed when he wrapped his arms around me and swept me back off my feet like we were dancing. His lips touched mine, this time without the humor and with all the heat.

When he was done, he placed me back on my feet and gestured to his place. "This is it," he said. "It's kind of bare because I'm not here very much."

True, it wasn't overfull with stuff, but I liked it that way. The walls were the color of gray storm clouds and all the trim was bright white. The floors looked like old hardwood that had been re-stained a dark walnut shade.

The room was a giant square with a large tan leather sectional dominating most of the floor space. In front of it was a large square ottoman covered in the same fabric as the sofa. Off to the side was a small wooden side table littered with several remotes and a small lamp with a white shade.

Against the far wall hung a large flat-screen TV, and beneath it was a black TV cabinet. Beyond the living room was a wall with a large pass-through cut out, and I could see behind it was the eat-in kitchen.

Spencer stepped behind me and dropped his keys and gun onto a small table by the door. There was a stack of mail there that looked like it was collecting dust, and he kicked off his shoes, tossing them beneath the table.

He looked kind of silly wearing his jeans and his suit jacket with no shirt. I offered to give back his T-shirt, but he wanted me to leave it on, so I did.

He was still holding the small duffle of clothes that I packed, and he pointed to the room off the living room. "How about that shower?"

I nodded and followed along behind him into the single bedroom in this apartment. The walls were the same gray, the trim the same white, and the bed was huge. It was definitely a king size and the headboard and footboard were padded leather. All the blankets were white.

"Nice," I said.

"You seem surprised." He grinned and tossed my bag on the bed.

"I gotta say, I thought it would be more… bachelor-ish?"

He laughed. "For a long time, I didn't really have much of anything. I moved around a lot and deployed with the Marines. When I got out and moved here, I wanted something more… permanent. Something that felt like mine, you know?"

I nodded.

"So I bought furniture." He shrugged.

"I like it a lot."

"Wait 'til you see the inside of my shower," he said, coming up and wrapping his arms around me.

"And what is so special about your shower?" I asked.

"I'm going to be naked in it."

"Hmm," I purred. "Well, that's definitely special."

Spence laughed and dropped a kiss on my lips while yanking off my shirt. Then he kissed me again. He stepped back and unfastened his jeans, revealing the short, wiry curls at the apex of his hips.

When he held out his hand, I took it, allowing him to lead me into the all-white bathroom and turn on the shower.

What was supposed to be a *get clean and get out* activity turned into a slow exploration of every body part we both had. The suds were slippery, his hands were hot… and his mouth was even better.

By the time both of us were thoroughly "clean," the water had long gone cold, and I was shivering.

Spence reached around me to shut off the spray and palm my ass one last time. "You're fucking sexy."

"You're not so bad yourself."

He grinned and opened the shower door. I stepped out ahead of him, reaching for a fluffy white towel. I ran it over my face and head, then wrapped it around my shoulders.

The silence in the room seemed a little off, so I glanced over my shoulder. Spencer was still standing in the shower, dripping wet, with an angry expression.

"Spencer?"

"Why didn't you say anything," he ground out.

"About what?" I asked, confused.

His muscles flexed and bunched as he stepped out of the shower and pulled the towel off my shoulder, exposing my back.

"This," he growled, turning me toward the mirror. I had to look over my shoulder and into the reflection to see what he was talking about.

There was a blotchy purple bruise low on my back. "It's no big deal," I said, my gaze briefly touching on all the other bruises that marred my skin from the first attack my body endured. I tried to pull the towel back up, but Spencer wouldn't release his hold on the material.

"That wasn't there before," he growled. I watched as a stricken look came into his eyes. "Did I do this?"

"Of course not!" I hurried to say. "You couldn't be that rough with me if you tried."

"I didn't notice it," he murmured, brushing his open palm against it.

It was sore, but in truth, I hadn't noticed it either.

I'd been too busy enjoying his body. "At the house earlier," I said, remembering. "The intruder, he punched me around that area."

Spencer's eyes went flat. It made my stomach hurt, so I tugged the towel out of his grip and pulled it up around my shoulders. "It doesn't hurt," I said, wanting to take away the look on his face.

He reached up and grabbed the ends of the towel that met at my chest. Gently, he tugged it closer, and I was momentarily distracted by the way his damp skin glistened under the lights.

"I'm going to get this son of a bitch," he vowed. "He put his hands on you. For that I will kill him."

"Spence." I covered his hands with mine. "I don't want you to kill him. Because if you do, he'll successfully take away something that I'm pretty sure I can't live without."

"If he's dead, he can't hurt Jack either."

I shook my head. "I didn't mean Jack. Not this time."

"Then?"

"If you kill him, they'll put you in jail, and I'll have to live without you."

Emotion passed behind his eyes, and he pulled me against his chest. I curled in close against him, letting the moment absorb into my skin.

"I'm gonna keep you, too," I whispered.

He groaned and held me tighter. "I'm not going to let anything happen to you," he vowed.

After several minutes in his arms, I pulled back and gave him a smile. "As soon as the president is dead, the threat to me and Jack will be, too."

The same look from before, the dark, angry one he displayed at my house earlier tonight, resurfaced.

"Why do you keep looking at me like that?" I demanded. "What aren't you saying?"

"Get dressed. Then we'll talk."

I thought about protesting and making him lay it all out here and now. But some conversations were better held while wearing pants. This was probably one of them.

I left him in the bathroom to dry and get changed and wandered out into the bedroom to dig through my duffle. I pulled out a pair of navy leggings and a loose A-line tank top that was the same color of the walls.

Quickly, I brushed my damp hair and decided to braid it in pigtails again so it would be wavy in the morning for work.

Spencer put on a pair of tight black boxer briefs that totally stole all my attention until he pulled on a pair of low-riding dark-gray Nike sweatpants. When he pulled a T-shirt out of the dresser, I shook my head and he tossed it aside with a grin.

Shirts were not required for this conversation.

"You want something to eat?" he asked.

I shook my head. "I want you to talk."

He sighed.

"Why do you keep getting this look… this angry, shadowed look, whenever I say anything about your plan?"

He scrubbed hand over his face. "Elle…"

"Just say it, Spencer. I'm a big girl."

"The threat to your life isn't going to just go away when everyone thinks the president is dead." He rushed the words out like he couldn't bear to speak them.

"But he said…" My voice trailed away.

"He lied, darlin'. That's what murderers do."

I felt stupid. Of course he lied. What kind of person actually believed if I did what he said he wouldn't kill me?

Me.

I thought that.

Or maybe I was just in denial.

But now that I thought about it, I knew how ridiculous it was. Of course they wouldn't leave me alive. I was a witness. Someone who could put them away.

"They're going to kill me to keep me from talking," I echoed.

Spencer stepped closer. "They're going to try."

"And Jack?" I asked, hoarse.

"He's just a kid. I don't think they care about him. He's just a bargaining chip to make you do what they want."

"Who would leave a little boy without parents?" I asked, horrified.

He tried to hug me, but I pushed him away. I didn't need comforted right now. I needed this to be over.

"You have protection, Elle," Spencer said. "The Secret Service isn't just going to let these assholes get to you."

"But what if they do?"

He swore. I knew he hated this. The way he felt radiated off his body. It soaked the room with frustration. I hated it, too. But I also realized it was an advantage.

"That's how we can get them," I said.

His eyes snapped up. "What?"

"When they come to kill me. You can take them into custody then."

"No," he said, flat.

"Why not?"

"I'm not using you as bait."

"I already am bait."

He began pacing the room. "No," he said again.

I opened my mouth to argue. To tell him he wasn't my mother and couldn't just tell me no.

He stopped, held up his hand. "Remember how I said when I moved here, I wanted something that felt permanent. Something that felt like home?"

I nodded.

"I've been chasing that feeling most of my adult life, Elle. I bought this place, I painted the walls, redid the floors. I filled it with nice, comfortable furniture and got the address on my driver's license. I made this place somewhere I never had to move from."

"I understand that, Spence."

"No," he said, cutting me off. "I don't think you do."

I didn't argue with him. If he said I didn't understand, then I didn't. I wouldn't want someone telling me how I did and did not feel, and I wouldn't do that to him. I'd let him tell me.

"The truth is it didn't matter what I did here. This place… it never felt like home."

He ran a hand over his head, and the damp strands of his hair stuck out randomly with the movement. It made him look vulnerable and endearing all at once.

Spencer looked up. His eyes were sincere. "You feel like home to me."

His words seared me, branded me, claimed me.

"I thought a home was furniture and paint. I thought it was an address you didn't have to leave. Maybe for some people, it is. But not for me. You're it for me. You can't ask me to put that in jeopardy. I will not put *you* in jeopardy."

There was nothing.

Nothing I could say that would ever be more beautiful than that.

Nothing I could say to change his mind. In fact, after that, I didn't want to change his mind. For the first time in my life, I was seeing myself through someone else's eyes… and it was amazing.

"Okay," I said. It was lame and stupid, but I had no clue what else to say.

"Yeah?" he asked. Vulnerability shone in his eyes.

It was a new look for him.

I closed the distance between us, slipping my hands around his tight, narrow waist. "Did you really think I could say anything else?"

He grinned crookedly. "I hoped not. That was the best I got."

"Thank you, Spence," I whispered, tipping my head back to look up.

"For what?" he asked, his brows drawing down.

"For coming home."

He kissed me slowly. The strokes of his tongue went deep. His full lips were lazy in their exploration, and he nibbled at my lips gently, enticing me to melt against him completely. When I began to feel dizzy from his intoxication, Spencer lifted me and spun. My back went against the wall and my legs wrapped around his waist. He smiled and kept kissing as I plowed my fingers through the damp strands of his hair.

"You're going to stay here," he said, lifting his head. "With me, until this is over."

"But that will look suspicious," I protested, resting the back of my head against the wall. "Whoever this is will think I told you."

"Let him." He shrugged. "If he really is on the inside, he already knows anyway."

I really didn't want to stay at my place anyway. "I guess it will give me time to fix the window."

A slow smile spread across his face.

"But don't get any ideas. As soon as Jack comes home, I'm going back to my place."

"Fine. I'll stay with you." He dipped his head to kiss me again, but I turned my cheek.

"I will not be parading men in and out of my house in front of my son."

"Not *men*. Just me," he countered.

"I'm serious, Spencer," I said, pinning him with a stare. He realized I was being serious and this was important to me. "I can't let you be there all the time. It will confuse him…"

"Can I sneak in when he's in bed?" he asked.

Clearly, he was good at compromise.

Or maybe I just really, really liked him.

"That could be arranged."

He dipped his head to kiss me again. I turned away, again.

He groaned.

"You understand, right?" I worried. Now that I knew Spencer was going to be in my life, I felt this sense of urgency to make him understand that I had to put Jack's needs before my own.

"I understand, darlin'," he drawled. "You're just doing right by him. I respect that."

"You aren't mad?"

"I will be if you don't kiss me."

I kissed him.

Not once, but twice.

After we'd fixed a couple of fast sandwiches in just the glow of the light from the fridge, we climbed in the giant bed in his room. My limbs were tangled around his, my cheek pillowed on his chest as the sound of his silent breathing filled my ears.

I couldn't sleep. Not because I didn't feel safe and not because I wasn't in my own bed. I couldn't help but think about what Spencer said. How he refused to use me as bait.

I wondered if he would have a choice.

20

Being back in the kitchen felt good. I was in my element here. The sound of meat searing in a pan, the process of chopping fresh vegetables for a perfectly seasoned medley, and the usual chaos of the kitchen environment were all music to my ears.

Most creative types were thought of as singers, writers, painters. But I was an artist in my own right. I designed dishes that not only pleased the eye, but the palate as well.

One of the reasons I liked cooking so much was because I didn't have to play by the rules. Sure, there was always a recipe to follow. But I could add a dash of this and a dash of that and experiment. Sometimes the results were awesome, and sometimes they were horrible. But it was okay. I could always dump out the awful and try again.

I also loved to watch other people enjoy the food I made. It was like serving them a little piece of myself and them loving it. It gave me a deep satisfaction to know I was good at something, something I worked so hard for.

The last couple years hadn't been easy—going to school, holding down sometimes two jobs at a time. I worked in kitchens all over D.C. I waited tables. I washed dishes. I did every job there was to have in a kitchen. When I was pregnant with Jack, I had horrible morning sickness and the sight of food made me want to puke all the time.

But I made it through.

I prepared the dishes. I experimented with new flavors and menus. I earned a reputation for being a young master with cuisine.

When I got a callback for the position here at the White House, I was stunned. Working for the first family was a high honor, and being considered at such a young age was even better. I worked a lot of long hours those first couple months. I had to prove myself. I had to earn the respect of the others in the kitchen.

I sacrificed some time with Jack, a lot of sleep, and my entire social life. In the end, it was worth it. I got to do what I loved and make good money doing it. Yeah, the hours were long, but not so long that I still didn't have time with my son.

I missed him.

I missed him every second of every day. I wondered where he was, who he was with. I wondered if he missed me, if he was confused. I wondered if he would look bigger when I saw him again.

And I would see him again.

I hadn't worked this hard, swam uphill for this long, to lose it all now.

I was nervous about the plan. Some of the details were still being worked out. Very, very few people were being told about this information. Spencer and I barely saw each other during the day. Not like before. He was usually shut up in Walsh's office, making plans and going over everything a million times.

I missed him, too. Yeah, I saw him daily. I spent my nights in his bed. I can't say we got much sleep, but when Spence was around, it wasn't sleep I wanted. My body tingled just thinking about him, and I forced my thoughts away from the bedroom and focused on what I was doing.

Making cookies. Chocolate chip.

The jar needed refilling, and well, if I was totally honest, I hoped Spencer might somehow sense I was making his favorite and come snooping around to steal one.

As I was sliding the last few cookies off a baking sheet and onto the cooling rack, voices drew closer, one that wasn't familiar to the kitchen staff, so I glanced up.

The vice president's aide was walking through the kitchen, discussing something with the manager. Both of them had their heads bent over a clipboard and were discussing whatever was on the paper.

As they walked by the island I was working at, Mr. Caroway stopped and smiled. "Elle!" he said. "Those smell divine!"

He was wearing an expensive three-piece suit in navy blue with a gold tie. His salt-and-pepper hair was combed neatly back away from his face, making him appear sophisticated.

"Thank you, Mr. Caroway. Please, help yourself."

He snatched one up off the counter and bit into it. Melty chocolate clung to his lips as he chewed. Sounds of appreciation came from his throat as he took another bite. "Best cookie I've ever had," he said.

I laughed. "Thank you."

Clearly, he wasn't afraid of my cooking. When I first started back in the kitchen, I was afraid everyone would react like Langdon and not want to eat anything I touched. So far, no one said or did anything that made me think they were suspicious. In fact, it seemed no one knew about what was going on at all. The Secret Service was clearly very good at keeping secrets.

"We were just going over the menu for the big dinner coming up," he said, motioning toward the kitchen manager.

"I hope everything is to the vice president's liking," I said.

"Oh yes, everything looks wonderful."

"I'm glad to hear it," I said, pushing another cookie in his direction.

He grinned and picked it up.

"Elle is the one who created the menu for the dinner," the manager told Mr. Caroway.

"Is that so?" he asked.

I nodded. "Yep. I plan almost all the dinner party menus here."

"Well, if the rest of the dishes at the dinner are as good as these cookies, then I declare the night will be a great success!"

"Do you mind if I take just one more?" he asked, reaching for another cookie.

"As long as you leave me some," Spencer said, stepping into the kitchen. I couldn't stop the grin from splitting my face. He reached out to shake Mr. Caroway's hand and winked at me over the man's shoulder.

"How's it hanging, Felix?" Spencer asked.

"Buried under paperwork," Mr. Caroway replied. "Figured I deserved a cookie break."

"I like your way of thinking," Spencer said, shoving an entire cookie in his mouth.

I shook my head. You'd think he'd use his manners.

"Well, I better get back to it," Felix said. The kitchen manager inclined her head. "I look forward to sampling the menu," he told me before turning away to leave.

When he was gone, Spencer looked at me with raised eyebrows.

"What?" I asked.

"You sharing my cookies with other people?" he asked, coming around to my side of the island.

I laughed. "I didn't know they were exclusively yours."

He caught me around the waist and towed me in to him. "Oh, they're exclusive," he murmured. "The only man reaching his hand in this cookie jar is me."

He made a growling sound and kissed me swiftly. Then he shoved another cookie into his mouth.

"I knew making these would get you in here," I said, amused.

"You miss me?" He smiled.

"Maybe." I sniffed.

"I miss you, too."

He caught me around the waist again and pulled me close. "It's almost over," he whispered against my ear.

Nerves bunched in my belly, but I forced them down. The plan was in place. We were going through with it. I wanted my son to come home.

"I miss Jack," I said quietly.

"I know, darlin'," Spencer said. "He's doing good. I promise."

"Can't I just talk to him?" I asked. It wasn't the first time.

He groaned. "You know how hard it is to say no to you?"

"You could say yes." I tried.

Spencer grabbed me by the waist. "Give me two days. Three tops."

The dignitary dinner was the day after tomorrow.

"You really think things will move that fast after…?" I kept my voice low.

Someone walked by and Spencer covered up our conversation by kissing me. Apparently, PDA was a good way to look inconspicuous.

I heard some muffled giggles fading, and Spencer pulled away. As usual, he dropped a quick second kiss to my lips. "Thanks for the cookies, babe."

He shoved another in his mouth and picked up at least four more.

I knew our conversation was over. We weren't supposed to be talking about anything here anyway.

"Elle." The kitchen manager appeared. "Could we go over some last-minute changes and additions to this menu?" She held up her clipboard.

"Of course," I replied. "Mr. Caroway requested changes?"

"On behalf of Vice President Snyder."

I gave Spencer a small smile and he winked. "Catch ya later," he said.

"Bye," I called, going back to work.

As the changes were outlined to me (they were fairly minor and easy to accommodate), this odd feeling came over me. Sort of like a terrible foreboding, like my subconscious was trying to tell me something.

But how could it tell me something it didn't really know?

It couldn't.

I just hoped by the time I figured it out, it wouldn't be too late.

21

By the evening of the dinner, I was strung out. My nerves were frayed, and I just wanted this to be over, one way or another. It seemed like the anticipation of this situation was turning out to be far worse than the actual act.

I hoped anyway.

Spencer seemed distracted, going through profiles of the White House employees over and over again. They added extra secret security to the event and were disguising them as guests. He told me not to worry.

I worried anyway.

Thankfully, I couldn't stress too much because I was too busy in the kitchen. Preparing a sit-down dinner for a ton of people required most of my attention.

The main course was comprised of rack of roasted lamb, roasted garlic asparagus, and creamy chive mashed potatoes. Before the main course, we were serving chilled melon soup and a mixed green salad with homemade balsamic vinaigrette. There were crusty French rolls in the warming drawer, freshly whipped sweet butter, and tons of wine.

For dessert, we chose to serve something light, strawberry granita with mint and shortbread cookies.

Very few people knew about what was going to happen tonight. Me, Spencer, Walsh, and two other Secret Service members. I was supposed to "poison" the president with dessert.

That meant I had to sweat the entire dinner, waiting.

These dinners were not short affairs. They lasted for hours. I understood they were necessary and part of the political world, but my God, they were boring.

As the chef, I needed to be present in case issues came up with the food, adjustments needed to be made, etc. So it wasn't unusual for me to be here in the kitchen during the dinner.

I hadn't heard from the men who were threatening me since the night at my apartment. But I didn't need to see them to feel the threat hanging over my head. There was a clock inside me, ticking… reminding me that tonight was my deadline.

Please let this work, I prayed for the millionth time.

Spencer was here, too, but I didn't see him. He was doing his job and I was doing mine.

When dessert finally came around, my entire body ached from my muscles being so tight. I was only too glad to prepare the president's dish and carry it, by hand, out to the server. "This is the president's," I told her.

She nodded and took the dish, presenting it to him right away.

He took it with a large smile and then joked good-naturedly with the man sitting at his side. He seemed so laidback, so relaxed that my stomach knotted.

What if he didn't go along with the plan?

What if he had his own agenda?

He seemed far too comfortable for a man who was about to "die." I prayed it meant he was just a really good actor.

Once all the dessert was passed out among the guests, everyone began to eat. With bated breath, I watched from behind a cracked doorway as the president picked up his spoon.

"Delicious," I heard him tell the First Lady as he took a second bite.

My teeth sank into my lower lip, and I watched the unfolding scene. Spencer stood not far away, looking like a statue, standing tall and stock-still. His face gave away no indication he knew what might happen.

No one did.

Seconds ticked by. I felt sweat dampen my brow.

The president's spoon clattered against the plate holding his dish. He smiled tightly and wiped at his brow. The First Lady leaned into his ear, asking him if he was all right.

I watched him assure her he was.

He got up from the head table, excusing himself. On his way to a nearby door, he stumbled, then righted himself. Walsh went to his side, assisting him in going out the door.

Just as the door was almost closed, I saw the president collapse on the floor. Spencer and the other Secret Service agents all received word in the black earpieces they were wearing. They filed out of the room quickly, barely drawing any attention.

The door opened and closed quickly as they all disappeared to the president's side.

A few guests at the president's table looked around in curiosity, worry marring their made-up faces.

How everyone in the room could just go on, how they could not even realize someone was falling ill among them, how a sinister plot was developing right beneath their nose—it amazed me.

After a moment, the First Lady appeared concerned. She excused herself and knocked on the door the president just left through.

She was admitted entrance.

Before the door latched, her muffled sobs broke through the hushed conversation that filled the room.

It was done.

22

It was announced the president would not be coming back to the dinner. He had fallen ill and was resting in his private quarters. His personal doctor was on his way.

Of course, it was implied that this not become common knowledge as the president just needed to rest and would be back to normal very soon.

The dinner continued. No one seemed overly concerned.

I went back to the kitchen because lurking behind doors looked suspicious.

My chest felt tight as I worked, covering what was left of the granita with plastic wrap. It was hard to not know what was going on. Where was Spencer? Was he okay? Were they able to get the president out of the White House undetected?

It made me realize that I knew very little about this plan. So many details likely went into this, details I wasn't privy to. It was Spencer's way of protecting me, the Secret Service's way of doing their jobs... but it still sucked.

When all the extra food was put away, I grabbed a rag and began cleaning some of the counters.

Marley, one of the kitchen staff, came rushing up to where I and a few other people were cleaning up. "Did you hear?" she asked, her face was pale and her eyes were wide.

We all paused and looked up. "Hear what?" I asked.

She sniffled. "It's horrible news."

"What is it?" someone beside me demanded.

The bottom fell out of my stomach. I knew.

"The president isn't sick," Marley said. "He's dead."

I knew it was coming.

It didn't lessen the shock.

It didn't dampen the reaction I had. The wet rag fell out of my hand and made a slapping sound on the tile floor.

"That's not funny," Mark, the man beside me, scolded Marley.

"It's not a joke," she said, her voice low and watery. "It's all over. Everyone is talking about it."

"But how?" I asked. "They just said he was ill."

"They think it was something he ate." She nodded as she whispered, her eyes wide.

"That's ridiculous," Mark said. "Everyone at the dinner ate the same thing. No one else died." He paused. "Did they?"

"Not that I know of," Marley said.

This was something I hadn't prepared for. Something I never thought of. The speculation. The rumors. In any workplace, people loved a good drama. They loved whispering by the water cooler. Well, this was about the biggest, most shocking piece of gossip the White House would ever see.

Of course there would be theories.

But those theories could come back on me.

We'll make sure you're the one who goes down for plotting to kill the commander in chief. The threat from the night that seemed so long ago filled my mind, taunting me.

Were these assholes going to get their way?

In an attempt to free myself of this crime, did I accidentally implicate myself?

"Then it couldn't have been the food," Mark insisted.

"Maybe someone poisoned it." Marley theorized.

I jerked like I'd been shocked. Both people looked at me. "That's impossible," I said, not even having to pretend to be horrified. "This place has a ton of security. We would know if someone on this staff wanted the president dead."

God, that was such an epic lie.

"Well, what else could it be?" Marley asked.

"Are you sure he's dead?" I asked.

Marley opened her mouth to respond, but the kitchen manager called for the attention of everyone in the room.

We all gathered around. It was evident by her tear-stained and pale face that she was going to tell us exactly what Marley already did.

"It is with great sorrow that I need to confirm the rumors already making their way through the White House. The president is dead."

Murmuring went through the room. Grief settled over the space like a suffocating blanket.

I didn't anticipate how horrible this part would be. How cruel this plan really was. These people, my co-workers, they all thought he was dead. They were grieving, mourning the loss of someone who wasn't really gone.

I knew I hadn't had a choice with this, but it still made me feel incredibly bad.

"The White House is issuing a gag order," she said, and I stopped listening. I knew what she was going to say. Everyone was being told to not breathe a word of this until further notice.

And me…

Well, I was just trying not call attention to myself.

"A thorough investigation is being launched immediately. Every member of the staff will be interviewed. Cooperate. Tell them what you know. Every detail can make a difference," she was saying.

When she was done talking, everyone went back to what they were doing. The atmosphere was subdued and heavy. I couldn't help but think about Spencer. The muffled cries I heard from the First Lady earlier tonight echoed through my brain, rattling in every corner of my mind.

Did she know about this?

They couldn't possibly allow her to think her husband had died.

Could they?

Some of the staff were called out to be interviewed. The kitchen was thoroughly cleaned. Some of the food from the dinner was taken away for testing.

My stomach roiled and threatened to empty itself on more than one occasion.

Thankfully, I didn't have to put on a brave face. I could feel everything I was and let it show. Everyone just assumed it was grief.

It wasn't grief.

It was guilt.

The hour drew late. Far later than I normally stayed. The staff began trickling out. Everyone's eyes were bloodshot and tired.

I was sitting at the island, just staring at my fingers, when a hand fell on my shoulder. I spun around quickly, hoping to see Spencer's face.

It wasn't him.

The kitchen manager frowned down at me. "Elle?" she asked. "What are you still doing here?"

I wasn't sure where else to go. I thought by now Spencer would have been around, but so far, he was nowhere to be seen.

"I was waiting to be interviewed." I lied.

She sighed heavily. "Ah, I see. Well, thank you for waiting. They're interviewing the wait staff now. It could take the rest of the night. Why don't you go home, get some rest? They will interview you in the morning."

"I can stay," I said, knowing I probably shouldn't leave.

"You look exhausted," she said. "Go."

I hesitated, not sure of what excuse to give.

"Is there another reason you want to be here?" she asked. The hint of suspicion in her tone was clear.

"Of course not," I said, standing up. "I just… This is just awful."

Her gaze softened. "I know. Get some rest. I'll see you tomorrow."

I nodded. She stayed, watching me. Like she was still suspicious of my presence. I had no choice but to grab my bag and leave the kitchen.

Out in the hall, people were milling about, whispering and crying. Spencer was nowhere to be seen, and I was afraid to go searching for him. I didn't know what he was doing, but I knew if he wasn't here, it was for a good reason. I didn't want to interrupt or get in the way of whatever he was doing.

Before I turned the corner toward the staff exit, someone stepped out into the hallway. I glanced up, hoping it was Spence. It was Mr. Caroway. His hair was mussed, his face was drawn, and the tie around his neck was loose and askew.

He saw me looking his way and inclined his head.

I lowered my gaze. The vice president appeared, looking completely shell shocked and distraught. Mr. Caroway put an arm around him and led him into another private room.

This plan was of huge magnitude. How angry would everyone be when they learned this was all just some giant ruse?

The summer air was cool because the hour was so late. My feet crunched across the gravel as I walked through the parking lot toward my car. I wasn't sure where I should go. My place? Spencer's?

I probably should wait for him, but hanging around would only make me look suspicious.

Man, I just wanted this to be over. I was tired and confused. I missed my son, my regular routine. My life.

At my car, I unlocked the door and sank into the driver's seat. I laid my head against the headrest and blew out a heavy breath. I tossed my purse on the floorboards of the passenger seat and reached out to turn the key.

That's when I noticed the small note taped to the clear plastic over my speedometer.

With shaking fingers, I pulled it off and slowly unfolded the white piece of paper.

Good job.

I crumbled the paper as a sob tore from my throat. This note meant two things:

1.) Whoever was responsible most definitely worked here.

and…

2.) I was no longer necessary.

23

I sat outside my house, staring up at it through the windshield of my car. I hadn't been here in several days. I was staying with Spencer, just like I said I would. I knew whoever was behind this knew. They seemed to know everything.

I wondered if they knew about our secret plot.

I hoped not.

I glanced back up at the house. The porch light was on, so was the lamp in the living room. I knew the window was fixed. Spencer had it done yesterday.

I probably wouldn't stay here tonight, but I could use some clothes and things, so I figured I could go in and get what I needed while waiting for Spencer to get in touch.

On my way to the front door, my cell phone started ringing. It was already in my hand and I hit the button immediately.

"Hello?"

"Elle," Spencer's voice filled my ear. "Where are you?"

"Hey." Relief poured through me. "I'm at my place. Just got here."

He grunted. "I'm on my way."

Before I could say anything else, the line went dead.

Inside, the house was just as I left it, but the air smelled slightly stale because no one had been here. I grabbed a bottle of water from the fridge and went upstairs to get a couple extra outfits and change my clothes. After I put on a pair of jeans and a short-sleeved white top, I went into the bathroom and washed my face and hands. My hair looked as limp as I felt, so I pulled it up into a high ponytail on top my head. After smoothing on some moisturizer, I went back into the bedroom and into the closet.

I couldn't help but think about the last time I was in here. When I was being drugged and attacked.

I wondered if that memory would always assault me when I was in here. I hoped not. This was my home. The only home Jack had ever known. It was a nice place with plenty of room, and I didn't want to move.

The front door opened and closed, and I stiffened. When I got to the top of the stairs, Spencer grinned up at me.

"Hey, darlin'."

"Hey," I said, smiling. It was good to see him.

He swept me up in his arms when he reached me, planting a kiss on my lips. "What the hell are you doing here?" he asked, setting me down after the usual second kiss.

"It was starting to look suspicious that I was still at work. I had to leave."

"Why didn't you go to my place?"

"I don't have a key."

He swore and pulled out a key ring. "Here," he said, taking off a silver key. "I have another at home I can use."

"This isn't necessary," I said.

"I want you to have it." Instead of waiting for me to take it, he stuck it into the front pocket of my jeans. "I have a key to your place."

Yeah, because he was having the window fixed. Still, I wasn't going to be asking for it back.

"Thanks."

"Sorry I took so long," he said. "I couldn't get away."

"Is everything…?" I began, not really wanting to vocalize everything that was going on.

He nodded. "It's good."

"Any leads?" I ventured.

His face drew grim and he shook his head. "Everyone there is acting the way you'd suspect. Nothing suspicious, and believe me, I've been watching."

I wrapped my hands around his waist and laid my cheek against his chest. He hugged me back, resting his chin on top of my head. I told myself not to freak out, that it was still really early. I mean, geez, had I expected whoever this was to be skipping through the halls in merriment?

A girl could dream, I guess.

"Come on, I'll take you to my place," Spencer said, releasing me.

"You aren't staying?"

His mouth drew into a line. "I can't. I have to go back to work."

I nodded. It was understandable. I grabbed a few things I needed and threw them in a bag, and then we left, locking the door behind us.

I walked toward my car, but Spencer caught my hand. "Just leave it. Ride with me. We'll come back and get it tomorrow."

"If you need to go back, I can drive myself."

"I want to spend some time with you," he replied. "Even if it's only a few minutes."

I smiled, but then the worry behind his words intruded. "Is everything really okay, Spence?"

"Yeah," he said, but it wasn't that convincing.

"Spencer," I said, digging my feet into the pavement. "What?"

He scrubbed a hand over his face. He looked tired and strung out. I felt guilty for pressuring him, but not guilty enough to keep walking toward his Mustang.

"It's probably nothing," he muttered. "It's just talk."

"Ahh," I said knowingly. "You heard the rumors."

His eyes flashed up to mine. "You did, too?"

"Of course. Work is a breeding ground for gossip, don't you know?"

"Fuck," he swore. "I thought we were supposed to be adults."

"Adults are worse than teenagers."

He grunted.

"I guess it is a natural assumption to draw," I said. "I mean, he was eating at the time he grew sick and then died."

"And no one else has been sick," he said, grim.

"They took samples of the food to test for poison," I told him. He nodded like he already knew.

"You think it will come back on me," I said.

"I don't know. I hope the hell not."

I began ringing my hands anxiously.

Spencer gripped my shoulders and looked into my eyes. "Look, even if you are suspected, it won't go anywhere."

"It won't?"

"Of course not. We know the truth. They can't pin you for a crime you didn't commit. Walsh knows it, too."

"But what about the investigators that have been called in?" I wanted to know.

Spence shook his head. "They're in the dark. They have to be for now. We need this to look legit."

"I understand."

"Look, when they interview you, just play along, answer as honestly as you can without giving anything away."

"And if they suspect something?"

His jaw muscles clenched. "Let them."

"What?" I was surprised he would suggest such a thing.

"We don't have a choice. Let them suspect you. When we catch whoever is behind this, you'll be cleared."

My limbs began to tremble. I was exhausted and afraid. I was reaching the end of my limit. I knew this shouldn't be a big deal, that it would all be cleared up, but even just the thought of being suspected of being capable of murder made me sick inside.

"It's going to be okay." Spencer assured me. "I got you."

I shivered.

He sighed. "Come on, let's get you to my place."

He pulled away, and when I didn't immediately follow, he turned back to take my hand.

Immediately, everything changed.

The air around us dropped ten degrees. Everything about Spencer froze.

"Elle," he said, his voice hoarse and afraid.

He was staring at me like he couldn't believe what he was seeing. I followed his gaze, looking down.

There against my white top, glowing in the inky night…

Was a red dot.

A laser shining directly on my chest.

I thought of the note. Of how I was no longer necessary.

They were eliminating me before I could be dragged in for questioning, before I could give away any information.

Both of us stared at the seemingly harmless red dot signaling the end of my life.

I dragged my eyes away and up at Spencer, at the man I loved.

The stark fear I saw in his eyes ripped at my heart.

And then everything happened at once.

24

The sound of a gun being fired, of a bullet whizzing through the air, was deafening.

"No!" Spencer shouted and threw himself at me.

His broad body shielded mine as he knocked me to the ground.

"Spencer!" I screamed and tried to shove him away.

But it was too late.

I slammed into the pavement and turned in time to see Spencer jerk when the bullet hit him. I let out a strangled cry, and he stumbled. I leapt up to support his weight, but he shoved me back onto the ground and righted himself, hunching forward, still trying to shield me.

"Get down," Spencer grunted.

I reached for him, tears falling down my cheeks. "Spence."

Another bullet hit the pavement just inches from where we were. Bits of blacktop burst upward, hitting against us.

"Move!" Spencer yelled and wrapped an arm around my waist, towing me up. We ran the couple feet to his Mustang, and Spencer shoved me behind the car.

I scrambled up to grab at him as he slid down the door, lowering himself into a sitting position.

His hand was pressed against his side, and his lips were turned down. I pulled off my shirt immediately and pushed at his bloody hand to press the fabric against the wound.

"You shouldn't have done that," I said, my voice wobbly. "We need to call an ambulance."

"I'm fine," he muttered.

"You got shot! You're bleeding!"

"The bullet just grazed me. You pulled me out of the way," he said, giving me a little grin.

I didn't care what he said. He was not okay. Blood was already saturating my T-shirt, and it was smeared across his chest. The white dress shirt he was wearing was completely stained red. I could feel the sticky warmth of his blood coating my fingers, and it made me want to scream.

"Harder, darlin'," he said, putting pressure with his seriously bloody hand over mine, showing me how hard to press.

"This is why I'm a chef," I muttered, peeking around the edge of the car. "The only emergency in food prep is when a dish is in danger of no flavor."

"Aww, your dishes never have that problem," he drawled.

How the hell could he be so charming as he bled all over my street?

"You at least need stitches." I worried.

"We need to get the hell out of here," he muttered. "They might still be here."

"They couldn't possibly still be here!" I said, outraged.

"They didn't make their shot."

His voice was deadpan. Matter-of-fact. It made my blood run cold.

As if to punctuate his words, another shot rang out. One of the windows of the Mustang shattered.

Spencer stiffened and dug a set out keys out of his front pocket. "We gotta get out of here."

I nodded.

Now wasn't the time to freak out.

I snatched the keys from him and reached up and opened the passenger-side door. "Can you climb in? Sit on the floor."

"Yeah. Climb across to the driver's seat."

I nodded and started moving. He snatched me back. "Stay low, darlin'."

"I will." I promised.

He pressed a quick kiss to my lips. "Go on."

I scrambled across the seats, trying my hardest to stay low. Glass from the shattered driver's window cut into my skin, but I ignored it. Behind me I heard Spencer getting into the car as I slid the key into the ignition.

I slid the seat all the way back as far as it could go and sat on the floor. It was uncomfortable as hell, but I managed to get the car started using my feet on the clutch and the gas.

"You couldn't have gotten an automatic?" I muttered.

Spencer chuckled. "My bad."

"You ready?" I asked him. He looked uncomfortable and in pain squished on the floor of his car.

"Go," he said.

I sprang up, threw the car in drive, and peeled out. I took out the mailbox on the way, but I didn't stop to see what kind of damage it made.

"Respect the car!" Spencer groaned as I sped down the street.

Another shot blew out the back windshield, and I screamed.

"Fuck!" he roared, and I increased the speed, tearing around the corner.

I kept my eyes on the rearview mirror, waiting for a car to fall behind us.

But one never came.

Spencer pushed himself up into the seat and pulled out his phone. As soon as someone answered, he began reporting about what happened, about shots fired and what direction they came from.

I was amazed. How the hell did he know the location and direction of the shooter? I was sitting over here proud I hadn't peed my pants and I was driving this stick shift without stripping the gears.

"What did the guy watching the house see?" Spencer demanded.

He let out a string of cuss words a few moments later. "You should have left a watch here!" he roared.

"Calm down," I told him, worrying about his blood loss.

I heard a voice on the other line but couldn't make out what he was saying. Spencer grunted a couple times, and I peeked beneath my shirt he was pressing against his wound and became anxious all over again when I saw the blood wasn't slowing down.

I imagined the man on the phone wanted to know where we would be.

"I need to go to the hospital," he said reluctantly. "I got shot."

Muffled yelling from the other end of the line made me grin. Spencer needed to get yelled at. He acted like getting shot wasn't that big of a deal.

"Yeah," he said after his lecture. "See you there."

When the call was disconnected, he jammed the phone back in his pocket and looked at me.

"Please don't die," I said, the choked words bursting from my mouth before I could stop them.

"Hey," he said, covering my hand on the stick shift with one of his red-stained ones. "It takes a lot more than this to kill a guy like me."

A sob ripped from my throat as the pressure in my chest built. He gave my hand a squeeze. "I'm okay, baby. Just get us to the hospital."

But it wasn't okay. "You shouldn't have done that," I said. "You should have let them shoot me instead."

He grunted. "I'd rather get shot than live without you."

"Getting shot is *not* a romantic gesture," I scolded, even though he totally owned me.

He chuckled.

I ran up over a curb, and the car in the other lane honked madly at me.

"I'd like to arrive at the hospital without further injury," he said, dry.

I gave him an evil look and the car went over a bump. He winced and fear flooded me anew. I gripped the steering wheel tightly and fastened my eyes on the road. The hospital was just up ahead.

That should have been me sitting there bleeding.
It's me they wanted dead.
I wondered when they would try again.

25

The hospital's bright fluorescent lights were jarring to my tired eyes. Spencer wouldn't let me drop him off at the emergency room door. Instead, he insisted on staying with me while I parked and then walked with me to the entrance.

He was absolutely maddening.

And stubborn.

But when he held my hand on the way in, I forgot to be mad at him.

Thankfully, when we got there, he was given first priority. It was a good thing because I was so strung out and worried that I would have gone postal on some poor nurse if they tried to make us sit in the waiting room for even five minutes.

Turns out, gunshot wounds rated attention immediately.

When I looked at Spencer as we waited for the nurse to wheel over a wheelchair (which he tried to refuse), I noted how pale he was looking. It worried me because he'd lost so much blood.

"You can wait here," the nurse said, eyeing my bra and blood-stained jeans.

I opened my mouth to tell her exactly what I thought of her prim instructions, but Spencer intervened.

"She stays with me."

"Policy states—" Hagatha started in her sour tone.

Spencer held up his hand and spoke, his voice hard and cold, leaving no room for argument. "She is a witness in a federal investigation. She's in danger, and I'm pissed off. She stays with me."

"Right this way," the nurse said and then led me down a long, white hall.

I made faces at her back as we walked.

What? Yeah, I was an adult, but I was in a bitchy mood.

She put us in a "room" that was sectioned off by a large curtain that hung from the ceiling. Spencer got up from the wheelchair as soon as she disappeared, and he stepped toward the exam table. I was at his side instantly, offering my frame for support. He didn't lean on me, but he did kiss the top of my head.

Once he was settled on the table, I began to pace. "I hope the doctor hurries up."

"I'm fine." He assured me. "A couple stitches and I'll be good as new."

"You lost a lot of blood, Spencer." I pointed out.

"This is nothing."

I stopped dead in my tracks. "Have you been shot before?"

"A couple times."

It hit me then. I realized that this was a man who was essentially in danger for a living. I guess I'd always seen him as the guy who stole cookies from the kitchen.

A guy who always flirted and made me smile.

But those things weren't his job.

His job was to protect the president. His job was to take a bullet for him if need be.

His words from before settled inside me. He wanted to be part of my life and Jack's. I wanted that, too. I wanted it more than I realized. Spencer hadn't really snuck up on me. He'd been there for quite a while. Since the first time he'd waltzed into the kitchen, looking for something to eat.

It had been almost a year since that day.

And I realized that year was always leading us here. The pull between us had always been there. We just hadn't been ready.

How was I going to live with the fact that he was in danger on a daily basis? How would I not worry myself sick?

"Hey," he said softly, breaking into my thoughts.

"Hmm?" I said, glancing in his direction.

"Come here." He hitched his chin at me.

I closed the distance between us, slipping a red-tinted hand against the shirt and applying extra pressure. His hand covered mine.

"I'm tough. I got this."

I cupped the side of his jaw with my hand, amazed at how fast my feelings for him grew once I allowed myself to admit them. He turned his head and pressed a kiss to the center of my palm.

It made me smile.

The doctor bustled in, breaking the moment between us, and I stepped away so he could look Spencer over.

He asked several questions, looked over the wound, and declared he needed stitches and an IV. I guess it really was a flesh wound. A bad one, but only a flesh wound.

When the doctor sent the nurse to get all the supplies as he set about getting ready to stitch him up, Spencer started to complain about the IV, and I swung around and gave him a look. It shut him up. Guess I was getting better at the mom look.

When they started giving him numbing shots and sticking the IV in the back of his hand, my stomach got queasy again. I went across the room and sank into the chair, averting my eyes from what they were doing to him. Instead, I looked out into the hall between the gap in the curtain that afforded us some privacy.

My eyes grew heavy as I sat there. All the adrenaline, stress, and lack of sleep was seriously catching up to me. When I finally did get to go to bed, I'd probably sleep for twelve hours straight.

My eyes were drifting closed when someone walked by our little room. He was walking at a turtle's pace and looked right in between the curtain. My eyes sprang open all the way as I watched him disappear out of sight.

Something about him was familiar. I thought I knew him.

I glanced over where the doctor and nurse were bent over Spencer, who was lying on the table, and I quietly slipped around the curtain.

Up ahead, a man with pressed khaki's and a dark-colored sport coat was continuing down the hall. Not far away, the hall ended, which caused him to turn back around.

He stopped when he saw me.

I did know him.

I rushed down the hall toward him, knowing he was here to get an update on Spencer.

"Mr. Caroway," I said, stopping in front of him. "I'm surprised to see you here."

"Hello, Ms. Bond," he said, inclining his head. "We are all very concerned about Mr. Waller. Word about him being shot has spread through the White House. The vice president asked me to come down here and get an update on his condition."

Something niggled in the back of my head. Something about what he said just didn't sit right with me.

"Of course," I said, realizing he was waiting for a reply. "Thank you for coming. I'm sure Spencer will be happy to know so many people are pulling for him."

"Are his injuries that severe, then?"

Why did that sound like he was hopeful? That strange feeling wormed its way through my chest. The whisper in the back of my mind turned into a scream.

"How did you know Spencer was shot, Mr. Caroway?" I asked.

"I told you," he said. "It's all over the White House."

"But Spencer wasn't shot at the White House. How would everyone there know?"

"Walsh, of course," he answered smoothly.

Wrong.

I knew, *knew* that Walsh would never tell everyone about Spencer. This shooting was part of the plot to kill the president. It was top secret. Walsh would never be that sloppy.

He cleared his throat to draw my attention. "Is everything okay?" he inquired. "Spencer?"

"Yes," I said, watching him carefully. "Spencer will be just fine."

A little bit of panic passed behind his eyes.

His icy blue eyes.

The dream flashed before me. The man with the ski mask and the icy eyes invaded my brain.

I gasped.

"It was you!" I burst out, unable to contain the reaction to figuring out who had been terrorizing me.

"I assure you I don't know what you are talking about." He sniffed, trying to step around me.

I couldn't believe I hadn't realized before. He was the same build and height of the man who broke into my home. He had the same deep voice.

Now I knew why he was so eager and non-hesitant to eat my cookies in the kitchen that day. He wanted to throw me off in case I was suspicious. He wanted to prove he didn't think twice about my food.

"You've been plotting against the president," I whispered fervently. "You shot Spencer!" My voice grew louder with the accusation.

"Shut up," he growled, menace dripping from every pore.

"I will not," I growled. "How dare you threaten my son!"

I turned to yell for help. Mr. Caroway grabbed my ponytail and yanked, making me yelp. He dragged me behind the nearest curtain and forcefully threw me into a rolling cart. The tray sitting atop went flying, clattering to the floor, and I fell. My knees took the brunt of my tumble. I grunted as pain shot through my legs, then pushed up to run for help.

He pounced on me, straddling my backside and wrapping his hands around my throat from behind. "I knew you wouldn't keep your mouth shut," he spat. "All you are is a loose end that needs cutting."

All four fingers of each hand pressed against my windpipe, threatening to crush it.

I gasped and gagged for air. He was going to strangle me if I didn't so something!

I blinked, trying to clear my vision and look for something, anything, I could use as a weapon.

"It's the perfect plan," he growled, squeezing just a little harder.

I began to wheeze.

"The president is dead. No one would have known why, and then my boss, the VP, would have had the position."

Did that mean the VP didn't know about this? Or was he the one behind it?

It was getting harder and harder to breath. My lungs seized, begging my body for air it wasn't allowed to have.

"But for it to stay perfect, you have to die."

"He's not dead!" I rasped, forcing the words from my throat.

The pressure on my windpipe immediately went away. I sagged against the floor, gasping for breath.

"What did you say?" he hissed.

"I said it was all a lie. The president isn't really dead."

I had no idea if I should be telling him all this, but I needed to buy myself some time.

"No!" He gasped, shock radiating through him.

I seized the moment and twisted out from beneath him, scrambling to my feet.

"Yes. And now that we know who's behind this, he can come out of hiding." I taunted.

His eyes were wild and unfocused. I felt like I was prodding a wild animal, and I had no idea how he would react.

My eyes focused on a silver instrument that must have fallen off the tray when I knocked into it. It was close to my foot, just within reach.

"I'll kill him myself," Mr. Caroway growled, straightening and taking a step toward me. "Right after I kill you."

"Is the vice president behind this?" I asked. I had to know the truth.

He made a face like he ate something spoiled. "Of course not. But I've been with him so long he would have brushed my little indiscretions under the rug. He would have made it so no one ever knew."

What the fuck was he talking about? This was all because he wanted to cover up his sins?

He lunged and I ducked, scooping the instrument off the floor.

I heard Spencer out in the hall, yelling my name.

I shouted out just as Mr. Caroway lunged at me again.

He collided with me this time, both of us going down in a tangle of limbs. I landed on the bottom, my vision slightly blurry from hitting my head against the tiles.

Immediately, I began to struggle against the thick weight pinning me down. I shrieked, afraid he would wrap his hands around my neck again. I never wanted to feel that way again.

But he didn't move to do that.

In fact, he didn't move at all.

His weight was ripped away, and Spencer appeared behind him. The heinously bright lights of the room were making it hard to see.

"Elle?" he said, still gripping Mr. Caroway by the back of his jacket.

I looked down.

The instrument was sticking out of his chest. Blood saturated the shirt around it.

"I stabbed him," I said, shocked.

"Fucker deserved it," Spencer said, letting go of him. His body made a smacking sound against the tile, and Spencer reached for me.

On my feet, I wobbled. My throat was burning, my head hurt, and I couldn't stop staring at the man I just stabbed.

Was he dead? I couldn't tell. He wasn't moving. He was lying there like a lump. This was the man who'd been terrorizing me. He was crazy.

Spencer grabbed my chin and pulled my face up. His mouth was moving, but I couldn't hear anything he was saying. He seemed to shout something over his shoulder, and a friendly looking nurse appeared.

I squinted against the lights, my head lolling back and forth. "She's going in to shock!" the nurse yelled and rushed away.

Spencer's arms wound around me, supporting all of my weight as I began to slide to the floor. My chin was titled back and something warm and moist covered my mouth. A rush of air forced its way into my starved lungs, and I gasped.

"That's it, Elle," someone said above me. "Breathe."

Another breath forced its way into my lungs.

After several long moments of gasping for breath, my eyes opened and focused on Spencer hovering above me with a drawn face. Had he been giving me mouth-to-mouth?

"Hey," I croaked.

"I can't leave you alone for two seconds, darlin'," he drawled, relief taking over his features.

"It was him," I said, my voice strained. "He was the one behind it," I croaked, trying to sit up so I could make sure he didn't get away.

"Shh," Spencer said, pressing me back down. Seconds later, a nurse came over and strapped an oxygen mask to my face.

"Just breathe," he said, brushing the hair out of my face. "He's still here. We got him."

I tried to speak but couldn't because of the mask.

"He won't hurt you anymore," Spencer vowed. "He won't hurt anyone ever again."

I knew then that I had killed him.

Tears gathered in my eyes and leaked down the sides of my face. Spencer gently wiped them away, but more continued to fall.

"You did what you had to do," he said softly. Then he picked me up off the hard floor and laid me on a nearby bed. "Everyone is safe now. Jack can come home."

I wanted to tell him everything I knew, about how I didn't think the VP was responsible, how he wanted something he did covered up. But every time I tried to talk, Spencer would shush me. The pure oxygen filtering into my system was welcome, and it didn't take long for me to give up. I could give him the details later.

A few minutes later, the doctor checked me out and declared I had a concussion. Then he turned to Spencer. "You ripped out the stitches I just put in," he reprimanded.

"Sorry, doc," Spence said, winking at me. "My girl needed me. I couldn't let her down."

The doctor began ordering people around for more supplies to redo his stitches, and Spencer returned all his attention back on me.

"So what do you say, darlin'?" he asked. "You gonna make time for me in that busy life of yours?"

I reached up and yanked the mask away from my face and smiled. I no longer worried about him walking out on me when the going got tough. We'd already been through hell, and he was still here. He was still gazing at me with love-filled honey eyes.

He was everything I'd ever wanted and never thought I'd have. I wasn't going to mess this up by pushing him away. Like I told him before, I trusted him.

"Kiss me," I murmured.

"Is that a yes?" he said, his dimples making an appearance.

"That's a hell yes."

He covered my mouth with his while the nurses in the room began fussing saying he was going to steal all the oxygen I'd just managed to replenish. I threaded my fingers into the hair at the base of his neck and pulled him closer.

The nurses continued to fuss.

We ignored them.

EPILOGUE

One Year Later…

I pulled the last batch of cookies out of the oven and set them on the stove to cool slightly before transferring them to the platter on the counter. Jack came running into the room, chasing the rambunctious puppy that Spencer bought him.

He said all boys needed a dog.

I think that meant he really wanted a dog and just needed an excuse to buy one.

I laughed as my little boy and puppy nearly tripped over each other as they played.

"Cookies!" Jack said, reaching up for one.

I laughed and pushed one closer to the edge of the counter so he could reach. "Don't give any to Bullet," I told him. "Cookies make puppies sick."

Out in the other room, the front door opened and closed. Bullet took off in a flash, barking and sliding all over the floor to greet Spencer at the door.

Jack laughed and looked at me with cookie all over his mouth. "It's Spencer!" I said, excitement rushing through me. Even after being together a year, he still managed to give me butterflies.

I heard Spencer laughing at the dog's antics, and then he appeared in the doorway, taking a deep breath of the cookie-scented air. "Cookies!" he said, echoing Jack's earlier word.

"Daddy!" Jack said and launched himself at Spencer.

Spencer's eyes met mine. Everything in me stilled. Time slowed. All the breath in me whooshed out.

Jack called Spencer daddy.

It was the first time he'd done it. The pure joy in the single word made my heart ache. Jack loved Spencer just as much as I did, and it was only natural he would assume Spence was his father.

The problem was Spencer and I hadn't had this conversation. I knew he was committed to us, to Jack, but I had no idea how he would feel about Jack calling him daddy.

Even clearly shocked, Spencer easily caught Jack and swung him up into his arms, giving him a big smile. "What 'cha got there?" he asked Jack, looking at the half-eaten cookie in his hand.

"Mommy made cookies!" he said and held the cookie out for Spence to take a bite.

He did and made a bunch of satisfied noises around the small bite. Jack laughed with delight, and my heart turned over.

"Do you want one, Daddy?" Jack said, his innocent eyes intent on Spencer's face.

I watched his Adam's apple bob in his throat. His eyes held so much emotion that it was almost painful to see.

"Jack," I said, stepping forward, wanting Spencer to know it was okay if he wasn't up for this.

Spence caught my eye and shook his head imperceptibly. Then he looked back at Jack. "I'd love one," he said, kissing Jack on the cheek.

He bent down to set the little boy on his feet. "You wanna grab me one, son?"

One word.

One three-letter word.

It obliterated me.

As Jack rushed off to do his daddy's bidding, I stood in the center of the kitchen and cried. Big, fat silent tears rolled down my cheeks as I watched Spence bend down and let Jack shove the entire cookie into his mouth.

Then Bullet ran back into the room, barking like a maniac, and Jack took off after him, his laughter echoing behind him.

Spencer stood slowly, chewing the huge bite in his mouth, and speared me with an intense amber stare. He prowled across the room, holding my gaze, and then reached out, wiping the tears from my cheeks.

"I think a father should be allowed to live in the same house as his son," he said, low, hooking an arm around my waist. "Don't you?"

I sniffled. "Yes," I answered, my voice watery.

"I love you, Elle," he said, brushing a kiss across my cheekbone. "And I love Jack. I'd hoped he'd someday think of me as his father."

"You are his father, Spence. You're the only father he's ever known."

"I think it's time we make it official, darlin'," he said, tipping my chin up with the backs of his fingers. "I think it's time you marry me."

Joy filled me up inside, and I couldn't stop my smile. "Don't you want to live with me first? Make sure you still like me?" I teased.

He grinned. "Nope. Don't need to. I'm already in too deep."

"I like you deep," I said, pressing a little closer.

He groaned. "Unless you want our son to see his mother in a very compromising position on this counter, you better not tease me."

"Our son," I whispered.

"Yeah, darlin', ours."

He kissed me, his lips lingering over mine while the salt from a rogue tear mixed between our lips.

"Daddy!" Jack called from the other room.

Spencer rested his forehead against mine. "I love that sound."

"Me, too."

"Let's get married this weekend," he said. "I don't want to wait."

"This weekend?" I pulled back, surprised.

He gave me that charm-dripping smile and turned up the dimples.

Of course I agreed.

It was the best day of my life.

THE END

Spencer's Favorite Chocolate Chip Cookies

INGREDIENTS
2 sticks of butter – softened (not melted)
¾ cup of light brown sugar
¾ cup of granulated sugar
2 eggs
2 tsp of vanilla extract
1 tsp salt
1 tsp baking soda
2 ¼ cups of all-purpose flour
1 bag of high quality milk chocolate chips
Chopped nuts such as pecans are optional.
(Spencer prefers without)

DIRECTIONS
In a large mixing bowl, combine the butter and sugar. Beat with mixer until combined. Next, add the eggs and vanilla extract. Mix until combined.

In a separate bowl, combine the flour, salt, and baking soda together.

Gradually beat the flour mixture into the wet mixture. Once all the ingredients are incorporated together, set the mixer aside. Add all of the chocolate into the batter and fold into the cookie dough with a large spoon or baking spatula. (If using nuts, add them now, too.)

Drop by rounded spoonfuls (Elle likes to use a small ice cream scoop for perfect measuring) onto a cookie sheet lined with parchment paper.

Bake the cookies at 350 degrees for 9-10 minutes.

Cookies will look slightly underdone when you pull

them out (but they will be perfect!). That's what makes them soft. It's what Spencer likes. Allow the cookies to cool on the baking sheet for approximately one minute and then transfer to a small baking rack or a sheet of foil.

Enjoy!

Elle's Quick Cookie in a Cup

INGREDIENTS
1 tbsp melted butter
1 tbsp granulated sugar
1 tbsp brown sugar
Pinch of salt
1 egg yolk
¼ cup flour
2 tbsp chocolate chips (mini's work great!)

DIRECTIONS
Mix all ingredients into a microwavable safe mug. Microwave for 60 seconds.

Serve to the cookie monster in your life!

Taste

Want more of the *Take It Off* series?

Look for **TRASHY** releasing August 2014!

Turn the page for an EXCLUSIVE reveal of the TRASHY cover!

Taste

She's trying to move on,
but the past won't let her go.

TRASHY

a *Take it Off* novel
CAMBRIA HEBERT

TRASHY

(a *Take It Off* novel)

She's trying to move on, but the past won't let her go.
I fell in love once.

It was a big mistake, but the biggest mistake of all was staying with him.

He pushed me around. He cheated and treated me like trash.

I don't feel sorry for myself, because I let him.

But no more.

I moved out. I'm saving my stripper's salary for an education that will get me somewhere better.

But breaking the chains of a shitty past isn't easy. He says I owe him. He says we aren't done. I don't care what he says anymore.

I do care about Adam.

But my history tells me I'm not the best judge of men. And the fact Adam's been married four times tells me he probably isn't a safe choice.

I need safe. I need better. I need out.

If the past is any indication of my future, getting out isn't going to be easy.

COMING AUGUST 2014

AUTHOR'S NOTE

You totally want a cookie right now, don't you?

LOL! Try the cookie in a mug recipe. It works! I've made it lots of times. Anyway, if you can hold on to your cookie craving for a few more minutes to read this here author's note, that would be great! I'll do my best to keep it short and sweet. Like a cookie.

Totally not helping, am I?

Ha-ha.

Anyway, this is the part of the book when I ~~bore~~ enthrall you with what I was doing and thinking while writing *Taste*. To be honest… I can barely remember. This summer so far has been a whirlwind of activity and deadlines for me. I originally wrote *Taste* as a novella. It was half the size it is now. I wrote it for *The Naughty Box 2*, which is an awesome compilation of short stories that a group of authors put out.

But *Taste* wasn't the first short I wrote for *The Naughty Box*. Nope. I wrote *Distant Desires* (part one) for the box. Then I fell in love with Tarek (the male lead) and wanted to publish it on my own as part of a serial series. So I wrote *Taste*, quickly. Like, I literally wrote 30,000 words in four days.

Then I fell in love with Spencer. And Elle. And the plot of this book. It nagged me. And nagged me. And screamed to be made into a full-length novel.

So… you see where this is going, don't you?

I have a serious case of Jekyll-and-Hyde syndrome, aka: I'm crazy and I pretty much drove my editor and the other authors in *The Naughty Box* cray-cray, too.

Anyway, I decided to write *Taste* into a full-length novel. So I wrote *Blank* for the anthology. *Blank* made it in the box, *Distant Desires* is out (sneak peek in the back of this book), and now *Taste* is a complete book.

All this happened in a month. Yes. I am insane.

I'll just call it my artist personality.

As many of my avid readers know, *Trashy* was supposed to come out next, not *Taste*. But Spencer couldn't be denied. So I wrote it. And now I am writing *Trashy*. I have another book chomping in the back of my brain called *Trace*, so look for that coming after *Trashy*.

Oh! And I hope you enjoy the exclusive look at the cover of *Trashy* in the back of this book, too! I LOVE this cover. The color, the shading, the image, it's so beautiful to me. I hope you love it, too.

Anyway, I would like to thank all of you readers for sticking with me, as my releases have been kind of cray-cray. The next few releases will all be *Take It Off* novels. I'd also like to thank you for giving *Distant Desires* a chance. It's getting great reviews, and it's a refreshing change from contemporary. Not that I don't love me some contemporary, because I do.

I hope you enjoyed *Taste*. It was a fun, fairly easy write for me. Spencer is a great character. I love his strength and humor. I think he's sexy and has a lot of tenacity. Elle was fun, too. She's the first character I've written with a child.

Okay, I will stop talking now. You can go get that cookie.

Or maybe two.

Or three.

See you next book!

xoxo **—Cambria**

Cambria Hebert is the author of the young adult paranormal *Heven and Hell* series, the new adult *Death Escorts* series, and the new adult *Take it Off* series. She loves a caramel latte, hates math, and is afraid of chickens (yes, chickens). She went to college for a bachelor's degree, couldn't pick a major, and ended up with a degree in cosmetology. So rest assured her characters will always have good hair. She currently lives in North Carolina with her husband and children (both human and furry), where she is plotting her next book. You can find out more about Cambria and her work by visiting http://www.cambriahebert.com.

Taste

BOOK BONUS!

Did you know Cambria Hebert writes beyond the *Take It Off* series?

She does!

Turn the page for an excerpt of
Distant Desires—An Erotic Tale from Beyond the Stars

by Cambria Hebert.

the abduction

It smelled like stale smoke and beer inside the overcrowded bar. Music that was popular about a decade ago and overplayed so much I wanted to scratch out my eardrums pressed in around me. Between it and the smell, I felt like I might suffocate.

Even though my shift was over, the place was busy enough that I would likely be asked to stay later, to help close down. Normally, I wouldn't even ask. I would just keep working. But tonight this place was getting to me.

My feet hurt, my head hurt, and if one more guy asked me if I moonlighted as a stripper, I was going to waste a good bottle of beer smashing it over his head.

Stupid college town.

Actually, it didn't even matter that there was a college in this town. It would still be stupid without it.

Born and raised in this tiny town in Maryland, I grew up with the right to say that. I wasn't sure of the population, but I knew it was minimal. We had a tiny mall where half the stores were closed because there just wasn't enough business to support them. The entire town breathed a sigh of relief when a big-box store moved in because, for once, no one would have to drive an hour just to get to one.

There was absolutely nothing to do here, which was probably why this bar was always crowded. When people were bored, they tended to drink. Not to mention the start of fall semester last week and the fact RoundRock was a block from the university made this place a popular watering hole.

Not that anyone here was drinking water.

I stopped at the end of the bar and waited for one of the two bartenders to make his way to where I stood. It was Matt. He'd been tending bar here since before I started. He was tall, blond, and looked like he was destined to become a doctor.

He wasn't going to become a doctor.

He played guitar, did shots under the bar when no one was looking, and drove a motorcycle even when it was raining.

Sometimes I teased him and said the reason he kept himself so clean-shaven and preppy-looking was because he didn't want anyone to know exactly how much trouble he was.

He never disagreed, so I knew I was right.

"You look like shit, Soph," he said, leaning across the bar to grin at me.

"You look like a life-sized Ken doll."

His grin grew even wider, revealing a small chip in the corner of his right front tooth. "Wanna be my Barbie?"

A squeamish feeling burst in my middle, but I ignored it. Matt wasn't interested in me. He never had been and he never would be. He was just a charmer who didn't realize the kind of effect he had on women.

Well, no. He did know. It's the reason he made such great tips.

He just didn't know I was also totally taken by his charm. It was something I never let him see. I wasn't about to turn into one of those giggling little ninnies that sat at the bar for hours, just waiting for him to smile my way.

Instead, I dished it right back. We'd fallen into a sort of friendship that way, sort of like I was the annoying kid sister he put up with because he had to.

In a way, it was a better deal than dating him. I actually knew him better and saw him more than any girl who went out with him. He wasn't the kind of guy to stick with the same lady very long. There were too many fish in the pond, waiting to be hooked by him.

"As tempting as it is, I think I'll pass," I shouted over yet another annoying song.

He placed a hand over his heart like he was wounded. I knew he was anything but. "Get out of here. Get some rest," he said.

"You sure?" I asked, glancing around the room again. "We're busy."

"I can handle it," he said, pulling a couple longnecks out of the cooler and sliding them down the bar to a set of waiting hands.

"Okay," I replied, untying my apron and tossing it on the shelf behind the bar. "I'll see ya later."

"Sophie," he called as I turned away.

My dark ponytail swung over my shoulder when I spun back around. "Yeah?"

"You sure you're okay?" Concern lit his caramel-colored stare.

He had the most beautiful hazel eyes. Sometimes they were green and sometimes, like tonight, they were the color of warm caramel drizzled over a sundae.

Ooh, ice cream sounded good.

"Yeah, I'm fine," I said. "I just have a headache."

Matt nodded and ran a hand through his already messy hair.

"Thanks for covering for me."

He winked at me, causing that fluttery sensation to reassert itself in my belly, before turning away to flirt with a blonde at the end of the bar.

I shook my head and left through the back, wondering how many numbers he would leave with tonight.

The rush of crisp autumn air against my skin was refreshing, and I took a deep breath, rolling my head on my shoulders to stretch out the knotted muscles.

The sky looked like liquid ink, dotted with a smattering of stars across the dark canvas. Mountains rose up out of the earth to jut into the night like great fortresses. When I was little, I always felt protected here because it seemed the peaks formed a shield around this town, carving out a little piece of safety in an ever-changing world.

Maybe that was why I never moved away. It wasn't like I hadn't thought about it a million times before. Even after I graduated high school and the opportunity to go away to college presented itself, I still chose to stay, instead attending the same university that many of the bar patrons inside did.

I realized I would likely always be a small town girl, but I was okay with that.

The gravel under my feet crunched as I walked across the parking lot toward my used Jeep Wrangler. It was an older model, white with a black ragtop that was slightly frayed around the edges. The seats inside were some kind of vinyl material, black to match the top. It didn't have air-conditioning and the controls were as basic as they got.

But it had new tires, working heat, and four-wheel drive. Those things were a must, considering the cold temperatures, snow, and mountainous terrain that was Frostburg, Maryland.

The ragtop was currently down, and I knew it was going to be a cold ride home, but I didn't care. Soon enough, I was going to have to strap on the top and leave it that way through the entire winter. I wanted at least a few more rides with the wind in my hair and the tingly feeling I got in my cheeks from the biting cold.

I tossed my bag onto the floorboard of the passenger seat and slid the key into the ignition. The radio blasted out of the speakers, and I jumped, immediately reaching over and shutting it off.

You'd think by now I would come to expect that. Whenever the top was down, I had to turn the music up really loud to hear it over the ripping wind.

But tonight was a no-music kind of night. Besides the headache that throbbed just behind my eyes and the tension coiled in my neck, I just wasn't interested in music tonight. I wanted to hear the rumble of the engine, feel every bump and jolt this old Jeep made over the road, and let the wind carry away every thought, care, and sound that came close.

It wasn't like I had anything to really be stressed about. My life was pretty good. I was a college student, had my own tiny apartment, a job, and friends. My parents were still married and lived just fifteen minutes down the road.

I wasn't trying to get away from anything specific. But sometimes a girl just wanted the open road, the silence, and nothing but the cleansing wind.

Before pulling out of the parking lot, I tightened the band holding my ponytail and pulled a Frostburg State hoodie out of the back and wrapped it around my body.

I took the long way home, driving down several roads I didn't have to, but choosing to because I liked cruising around. There were still people here and there on the sidewalks of Frostburg, their laughter floating into the open Jeep as I drove. On the side of Main Street was a popular coffee bar (it was popular because it was the *only* coffee bar besides the gas station) that looked like an old church. It sat on a little hill with cement steps rising out of the sidewalk to carry you up to a small green space dotted with outdoor tables. A group of college kids were exiting the arched door and laughing as the light turned green and I hit the gas.

After a while of just driving around, I glanced at the dash and sighed. It was after midnight. I had class at eight a.m. Time to go home.

My apartment was on the second floor of an old house that was converted into several apartments for college students. It was small, with only one bedroom, a tiny kitchen, a bath, and a living room. The rent was cheap and it wasn't too far from campus, so I considered it a good find. Only one other apartment in the house was rented, though, so I don't think many people agreed with me.

It stood down a narrow, single-lane road, kind of off the beaten path. True, it didn't take long to reach everything from my place, but it felt miles away from all the "nightlife" of the small town.

My headlights illuminated the single lane as I turned down it, gravel crunching beneath my tires. I imagined this used to be an old farmhouse, and the people who once lived here grew wildflowers along the roadsides. Big winding trees reached up into the sky and russet-colored leaves threatened to fall overhead and land in the seat beside me.

This road stretched about two miles before it gave way to the area where the house sat. The entire two miles were lined with long grasses, trees, and a wide view of the sky.

My foot pressed the brake and the Jeep obeyed, slowing a bit. I lifted my face upward, gazing into night. The stars were easily seen here because there weren't so many lights like all the other streets.

Beneath my hands, the Jeep stuttered. "What the hell?" I muttered and looked down at the gauges.

The headlights blinked out, shrouding everything in darkness as the entire vehicle shut down.

I wasn't going very fast, thankfully, so I just steered to the side of the road and braked, throwing the shifter into park. From there, I turned the key and nothing happened.

I knew I wasn't out of gas. I'd just filled up yesterday at the Sheetz near school. It hadn't been making any odd noises while I was driving, and I wasn't late on my oil change. Okay, maybe I was a little late on the oil change. Surely that wouldn't just make the thing shut off.

The headache behind my eyes decided to remind me it was there and pierced me with a sharp stinging pain. I sighed wearily.

I was only about a mile from my place. I'd just walk home and then call my dad in the morning. He'd know who to call to get someone out here to look at it.

After fishing my bag off the floor, I climbed out, not bothering to lock the doors. There was no point when it didn't even have a roof. Besides, there was nothing of value inside to steal, and unless they planned to carry the car away, I doubted anyone would be taking it.

I pulled the hoodie a little tighter around me as I walked and reached up to pull the band out of my hair, letting the dark-brown strands fall around my shoulders. Using the tips of my fingers, I massaged my scalp as I trudged down the road.

The sound of a plane flying overhead filled the night, and I pulled out my cell to shoot a text to my dad so he would see it first thing in the morning.

But the battery was dead.

Odd… I just charged at work.

I stuffed the useless phone into my pocket, muttering about how I couldn't afford to go buy a new one. Suddenly, an odd feeling washed over my body, something that seemed to penetrate below the surface of my skin and make my insides vibrate.

I noticed then that the sound of the airplane overhead wasn't fading away…

It was growing louder.

And it was unlike any other plane I'd heard before.

The ground underfoot began to vibrate, and I thought vaguely of an earthquake, but we didn't have those in this area. The sound overhead was like one of those annoying bug zappers, the kind that screeched when it caught its prey. It grated down my spine like nails on a chalkboard, and I recoiled.

My feet stopped hiking and I looked up, desperate to know from where that awful sound was coming.

My mouth ran dry.

My hair fell down my back and tickled my butt as my head tilted up to stare at the source of the sound.

I was seeing things.

The headache was causing me to hallucinate.

I was tired. Maybe I was coming down with something.

I blinked and swallowed hard. The little bit of saliva my mouth produced scraped down the back of my throat like jagged pieces of glass.

There was a giant disk floating overhead.

Like, for real.

If I had to describe it, I would say it looked a lot like a Frisbee, a silver one that seemed to hover high in the air without any help. It was much larger than me, blocking out my view of the sky and the moon.

As I stared, a few pulses of blue light blinked on and raced around the edge, like a little car on a track. There was a sound of metal scraping against metal as something in the center of the disk began to open, revealing a dark hole in the center.

"What. The. Fuck?" I said, staring at that black void. Fear skittered up my spine and snapped me back to reality.

I took off running, propelling my feet across the ground as fast as I could. As I ran, I glanced over my shoulder, swiping the wayward hair out of my eyes.

It was gone.

I practically tripped as I lurched to a stop.

I turned completely around, staring up at the empty sky. There was no little light. No bug-zapping sound. No giant Frisbee floating alone in the night.

I was insane.

Absolutely crazy.

I could never tell anyone about this. About the night Sophie Perez thought she saw a… a… spaceship.

A laugh burst from my chest.

I'd been watching too many reruns of the *X-files* on TV.

Then something behind me lit up, literally casting a light so bright it caused my body to create a shadow that stretched across the ground like I was suddenly seven feet tall.

My back stiffened.

It was eerily quiet—no sounds of an approaching car, not even the sound of the rustling wind. But the light couldn't be denied. It illuminated the green of the grass so everything appeared electrified, like a major thunderstorm ready to attack.

Slowly, I pivoted, the silence of the night causing an odd sense of panic to claw its way up the back of my throat.

The light was coming from overhead. Several yards away, it shone in a wide beam from the sky, revealing the road like a giant spotlight.

It was coming from that disk.

I blinked hard, but when I looked again, the image was still there.

It hovered in the air silently, no blue moving light, no annoying sound. If I weren't seeing it, I would have sworn nothing was there.

My breathing was ragged. My heart squeezed with great effort as it stuttered from the intensity of its beating. The light blinked out and barely two seconds later it reappeared.

This time it didn't just light the road.

There was something else. *Someone* else.

I opened my mouth to scream, only no sound came out. I lifted my leg to run, but it didn't obey. I was frozen where I stood. The only thing about me that worked was my brain, and right now I wished it didn't.

I'm going to die.

I'm going to die a horrible death and no one will ever know.

The silhouette in the center of the light began walking toward me. Sort of. It was more like it floated over the ground, hovering just over the gravel, gliding gracefully through the air.

I willed my body to move, to get the hell away. Still, my stupid body betrayed me.

I was a prisoner inside my own skin.

As the thing moved, so did the light and the disk overhead. Simultaneously, they all approached as one, drawing closer and closer until I was sincerely afraid I was going to pee my pants.

The being was wearing a silver robe with an oversized hood that shrouded its face. They weren't much taller than me, so I would guess them to be about five-eight or so. Of course, maybe if they were actually standing on the ground, they would be shorter.

I tried to call out, to beg for my life.

My voice didn't work.

It was as if everything around that disk was completely frozen in time.

The creature stopped before me, saying nothing, but I could feel the penetrating stare behind the shadows of the hood. Silently, it reached out its arm, the silky material of the robe draping toward the ground like a waterfall.

I tried to recoil, but it was no use.

Eerily long fingers with oversized knuckles reached for me. The skin that covered them was ultra pale and so smooth it looked like polished stone.

Two fingers wrapped around the skin just above my elbow. I imagined they would be icy cold, but they weren't. This thing's touch was much warmer than me. Even through my hoodie, I could feel the heat.

The next thing I knew, the sweatshirt around me was gone. Ripped away and out of sight. I felt myself swallow as fear flooded my limbs.

The fingers once again found the skin above my elbow. They were intensely hot.

It moved so achingly slow, trailing those too-long fingers down the curve of my elbow, down the sensitive flesh of the inside of my arm. If I had control of my body, I would have shuddered.

Then the fingers threaded through mine, a possessive action. This being seemed to claim my hand.

You can't have that! my mind screamed.

"Yes." The creature in the robe spoke aloud. "You are mine."

A single tug on our joined hands set my body in motion. I spilled forward even as my insides recoiled.

The light grew brighter, so bright I had to shut my eyes.

I felt something wrap around my body and support my weight because I no longer could. A feeling of lightness came over me, and then my feet no longer touched the ground.

I forced my eyes open, looking up toward the sky. That black hole in the bottom of the disk was back. It was an unwelcoming void in the center of the neon light. My robed kidnapper and I were being towed upward, like it was a giant spider and I was now tangled in its web.

I had no idea what was waiting up there for me.

But I knew it couldn't be good.

Read Sophie and Tarek's story in full now!

Exclusively at Amazon

www.ingramcontent.com/pod-product-compliance
Lightning Source LLC
Chambersburg PA
CBHW061546210726
48287CB00006B/2096